THE LAST CITY

BOOK SIX IN THE DEADBLOOD SERIES

MARY E. TWOMEY

MARY E. TWOMEY, LLC

THE LAST CITY

Book Six in the Last Deadblood Series

By

Mary E. Twomey

COPYRIGHT

Copyright © 2022 Mary E. Twomey LLC
Cover Art by Emcat Designs

All rights reserved.
First Edition: February 2022

This is a work of fiction. Any resemblance of characters to actual persons, living or dead, is purely coincidental. The author holds exclusive rights to this work. Unauthorized duplication is prohibited.

This book is licensed for your personal enjoyment only. If you would like to share this book with another person, please purchase an additional copy for each reader. Thank you for respecting the hard work of this author.

For information:
http://www.maryetwomey.com

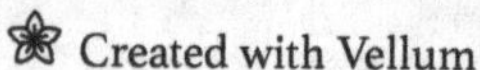 Created with Vellum

DEDICATION

To Cricket,

Who heals and loves without limits.

ABOUT THE LAST CITY

When it comes to finding a safe haven, Colette is running out of options.

Having a baby wasn't supposed to be possible, but now that Colette is pregnant, the happy couple isn't sure what to do. While Rome is ready to be a father, Colette knows the road ahead will be rough for the child she carries.

Being the Last Deadblood was supposed to ensure the violence against vampires would one day come to an end, but it seems that whether Colette draws breath or not, there are some who will always hate what they do not understand.

When war comes to their doorstep, Colette knows that if she does not put a stop to the revolution once and for all, her child will bear the consequences. Though it might take all she has, Colette will stop at nothing to take this stand...

...even if it might be her last.

"The Last City" is filled with political intrigue and scandalous secrets, written by USA Today bestselling fantasy romance author, Mary E. Twomey.

VOTING RIGHTS RALLY

It's odd to have no one's hands on my belly but my own. For the last eight months, it is a rare moment when there isn't a man treating my bump as if it's a crystal ball with mystical answers for the future.

The hallway behind the stage is narrow. Then again, I'm so big that even grocery store aisles seem narrow these days. It's been a long pregnancy, though, given that this is my first one, I'm guessing it's not all that different from the average woman's experience.

Swollen ankles aside, it hasn't been too bad so far. I'm just going to push that whole "giving birth" part of the equation out of my mind for the time being, since I have no idea how I am going to get through that.

A problem for another day.

Definitely not today. I have another month to go, so my little mystery baby is staying put for now.

I rub my hand over my stomach. The yellow silky shirt has just enough stretch to it so I can breathe, pairing well with the light gray slacks. The only issue is that the designer made the top backless, insisting that if my words weren't enough to make people pay attention, my outfit sure would. The yellow material is held together by a lacy string that Rome has had a fun time undoing with one of his deft hands. The back is wide open, giving the world a clear shot of my skin, along with the fact that I am not wearing a bra that can be seen from the back. The stylist that the designer sent over insisted my hair needed to be in an up-do, twisted at the back of my head to draw the eye to my long neckline.

I'm just happy I'm not overheating. This backless shirt idea isn't too bad.

Paulo, one of the security guards assigned by the governor, stands at the left side of the hallway, talking into his comm. "The Deadblood is in position. All clear on this side."

Normally I have Rome with me, along with either Nico or Orlando. After the world caught wind of the horror of Fintan murdering our father and escaping with the help of officers on the force in Mayfield, rulers from all over the world offered their shock and horror, but then quickly followed that up with help.

Paulo and Liesl are gifts from overseas. They report back to their country on the status of my safety. They make sure Fintan and his people cannot get to me. For larger events like these, there is a tightknit crew of security men and women out in the crowd on the other side of this curtain, scouring the throngs for signs of malfeasance.

For signs of Fintan.

I hate that this is what my family has become. My eldest brother and I were never especially close, but I had no idea he was behind the kidnapping when I was fifteen, nor that he had designs to do it again—selling my deadly blood to the highest bidder.

I straighten, rolling my shoulders back. "Not today," I vow to myself. Fintan won't get to me today. It took a few weeks to coax me out of hiding, but here I am, giving speeches and campaigning for a better life for us all.

A better life for my baby.

The father of my child rounds the corner. "Are you ready?" Rome asks me, walking toward me after he ends his call and tucks his phone away.

He needs his hands free to rub my belly.

Sure enough, one hand moves to the base of my spine while the other migrates to my stomach. He leans down to kiss the bump because, you know, it's been a whole five minutes since he's done that. "I'm right here, little one."

Rome takes the time to kiss me gently, settling my nerves that always bubble up at these kinds of things. I love the way his mouth tastes. He tugs on my lower lip, sucking it slightly before releasing it with a satisfied smile. "Mm. Thanks. I needed that."

There is so much of Rome that I need these days. Even

rolling out of our bed is a struggle without help. Of course, the daily dose of his blood keeps the larger aches and pains at bay. The doctor keeps checking me for hypertension, given the stress I am under, but Rome's blood heals the broken parts of me, just like his kisses have healed the busted bits of my heart.

"You remember the drill?" Rome asks me.

"This is my fifth speech this week. I know how it goes. They announce me. I ignore all the questions about the baby. I give my speech, congratulating the world on granting vampires the right to vote."

Rome nods, his hand sliding up my bare skin through the gaping vent in the back of my shirt. "And where will I be?"

"Right beside me, which means life is good."

The corner of his mouth quirks, his full lips reminding me just how striking he is. I love the sharp angle of his jaw, his lean yet muscular build and the way his body curves around mine.

Rome's thumb swipes across my bare skin at the base of my spine. "And where are the emergency exits?"

I point to the two obvious ones and then motion to the less accessible one in back.

"Good. And how quick can I get this outfit off you?"

I kiss him once more. "If all goes well, the second after we lock the door to our bedroom."

"That's what I like to hear." He is wearing his standard Valentino man attire: black fitted trousers, a white dress shirt with the sleeves rolled and a silver belt buckle. All of it pairs nicely with his thick, black hair, which I just cut yesterday.

My lust pauses when I notice hesitation in his expression. "What's wrong?"

"Nothing." When he realizes that answer will not satisfy, his shoulders lower. "Nothing important. Orlando spotted Senator Washburn in the audience. I hate that he's here. He voted against vampires getting voting rights, yet he's here at our victory rally? He wants the photo op, like he's all supportive. Makes me sick." Then he shakes off his foul mood. "I'll get over it. See? Like I said; it's nothing."

"I hope the people see him for what he is."

"They never do."

I run my fingers along the sharp edge of his jaw. I love the way his ice blue eyes are fixed on me. They drink in my form without holding back his affection, which is always married with attraction.

It is a heady thing to be adored by a Valentino man.

When Paulo clears his throat and nods our way, I know that's my cue.

Rome squeezes my hand. "You've got this."

I slip off my flats and toe my feet into the stilettos I know will command the most attention. Even though this is not the time to be testing my balance or my sore ankles and back, it will only be for the twenty minutes or so that I can tolerate the press. Then I will go back to my flats, which are lined with fur and feel like I am walking on clouds.

I roll my shoulders back and don the breezy yet controlled expression which communicates to the world that I am in charge.

My footsteps are sure as I move from behind the curtain, taking the center stage without guessing at my mark. I know the spotlight will follow me. People will listen because I tell them to.

At least, that's what I tell myself.

There are thousands here today in the city's capital. They gape at me with varying degrees of wariness and wonder because I have done the unthinkable.

I am dating the head of the vampires, and by some twist of nature, I am now carrying his baby.

I am followed everywhere I go now, with people taking photographs and breaking out all their old wives' tales, trying to predict the sex of the baby.

I am not ready for that conversation. That giant exclamation point is reserved for family only for now.

I've lost count of how many officials are here, ready to listen to the speech I have memorized in anticipation of the bill going through. This is a celebration of the hard work we have put in over the past several months.

We did it.

The vampires have voting rights now.

But now that I am standing here, staring at the sea of faces who care more about being able to gape at me in person than they do about the people I am here to represent, my mouth is dry and my speech feels paltry.

I have been working on this bill for months, but now that the win has come, I wonder if anyone truly cares about vampires, or if they are more intrigued in the circus aspect of it all.

I have no notes in my hands, and decide on the fly that I don't need the podium, either.

The stage is mine, so I am going to own the entire thing.

"Good morning, and welcome to the era of regret and repentance."

Nope, that wasn't how my speech was supposed to start.

Rome's head snaps in my direction.

Even though my other mate is at the foot of the stage making sure no one gets too close, I can feel Orlando stiffening when I start the speech by going off-book.

My voice carries easily out over the sea of thousands, for which I am grateful. "Today is supposed to be a celebration. We finally pushed through a bill to grant vampires their right to vote. They pay taxes, just like us. They are expected to follow the law, just like us. Yet they have had no say in who represents them. Finally, they have that right, yet as I stand here, there are those in power who are working to cut the legs out from under this progress." I motion to the area where I know one of my most ardent opposers sits. "Senator Washburn, won't you please stand?" I wait for him to take the position of honor before I unleash. "Senator Washburn is working on an addendum right now to limit polling places in vampire territory. He would like there to be one polling station for the entire vampire populace, guaranteeing that not every vampire will be able to vote, simply because there will not be the hours in the day to process them all."

I can tell the audience is confused. They came here for a rally, to show their excitement for the bill that just passed.

To find out that their victory will have red tape and countless stipulations?

This is politics.

I press on, foregoing any semblance of cheer. "What about absentee ballots, you might ask? Well, that would be a welcome alternative, but for the senator's addendum, which would limit vampire absentee ballots to those with a doctor's note. Being that they don't have medical care at the ready, this does away with all absentee voting."

I will not pause for the shouts of "Boo!" that are erupting all around the massive auditorium. They are music to my ears.

"The addendum also requires a valid driver's ID, which, due to overpolicing in the West End of Mayfield, many do not have. So today I want to congratulate those forward thinkers who voted to grant vampires the right to be heard. But I also want to challenge you." I step forward, commanding the spotlight with sheer ferocity. "The fight is far from over. While for most of you who live outside of Mayfield, this is a problem that doesn't affect your everyday life. But for me, it does. I live in Mayfield, and have moved into vampire territory. The father of my child might not be able to vote to make sure the person in charge cares about our baby enough to protect him or her."

My baby kicks, as if on cue.

My hand moves to my stomach. "So while this is supposed to be a celebration, it is a pause. Today is merely a breath that we grant ourselves before we pick up the baton and resume the fight for equality." I look out over the faces that have gone from celebratory to hardened with purpose.

Good. They will need that determination if the world is going to evolve.

My voice carries while my baby kicks again. "I have one question for all of you: Are you tired of the fight?"

"No!" comes the resounding gong of enthusiastic replies.

It's a beautiful thing, the cries of the impassioned. I can only hope they last long enough to enforce the change we all crave.

"Then show me how you will protect the future. Show me how you will stand up against Senator Washburn and those like him. He is here today to cash in on being seen at this rally, but he votes against equal rights, like so many others! Show me that your minds and your hearts are open to change, and that you are ready to push forth the policies that must come if we are to call ourselves humane. I..."

I open my mouth, but at that exact moment, I feel something I am not supposed to experience for one whole month.

I was told I had a month. I'm not ready for what I am positive is my very first contraction. My belly hardens and the inside quakes like the echoes of something powerful approaching as it awakens.

Panic strikes my features. Before I can voice anything, Rome rushes to my side from where he stood behind me. His arm winds around my hips, bolstering me should I need it.

I don't think he knows my labor might be starting early, but he knows the quaver in my voice, which is all he needs to hear to move quickly.

Still, I continue with my speech as best I can with Rome by my side.

"Maybe you all don't have as much to lose. Maybe it's not your child who will be silenced if this bill is not left unadulterated. But I like to believe that you are the kind of people who care even about children who are not yours, because that's how big your hearts are. You don't care if a person is a vampire or a human, a boy or a girl. You care that there is a chance for kindness in the world." I stand my ground, willing my child to wait just a few more minutes. My eyes glisten with passion that is now mingled with fear.

I was supposed to have more time.

"I trust you all know how to give Senator Washburn a piece of your minds. I trust you know how to vote him out of office for attempting to silence those who deserve to be heard. He would make your protests and votes a struggle for nothing. He would take your voices and silence them if they don't preach the bigotry that got him elected in the first place." I rub my stomach. "My child deserves better, and so do yours."

My child rolls in my stomach like the baby is trying to breakdance.

I gasp, letting my panic broadcast across my face.

I am not sure how long I can keep up the façade of everything being business as usual.

"Now, if you'll excuse me, Governor Ingrid Mason is going to field any of your questions concerning how best to vote Senator Washburn out of office. She can walk you through how you can help those who have been ostracized and belittled under the guise of civilized behavior." I rub my stomach near the bottom of the bump, worried that I somehow need to hold my baby inside of me for just a little while longer, and perhaps I can achieve this feat by pressing my hand to my stomach. "I expect you will have this amendment thoroughly dealt with before my child is born. I also anticipate your passion for justice will rush the necessary changes because I am pregnant, and I can't do this all by myself. I need you to fight this battle for me for just a little while, so I can give birth and start a new legacy." Emotions aren't exactly a rare occurrence these days, but it still surprises me when I tear up, especially in public. "I need you to make sure there is room in this world for my child. I believe the world is big enough for us all, but you might have to prove that to yourselves, and to the policy-makers who vote as if it's not."

Rome's hand moves to my stomach, and as if on cue, my belly hardens and quakes again, tightening my insides with pain enough to take my breath away.

Rome's eyes widen as all color drains from his face. "Was that... Are you..."

"Governor Ingrid Mason, everybody." I introduce her to the stage and grip Rome's hand tighter than a lesser man might be able to tolerate. We exit the stage at a leisurely pace.

Because I should have a month.

I'm not ready for this...

...Yet here we go.

2

THE ELEPHANT ON NICO'S LAP

My brother is the perfect person to have with me while I grit my teeth through a scream as we pull into the hospital.

"Breathe through it," Declan instructs. "You're holding your breath to brace yourself. Don't. Remember what the birthing coach said: breathing during a contraction will make for fewer issues when it's time to push."

I squeeze his hand tight while Rome races from his car to the hospital's entrance, requesting help, I hope. He's been gaunt and mute ever since we exited the stage of the rally to the tune of my contractions.

Declan opens the door for me, but I am afraid to let go of his hand, so he has to pause while I scoot to the edge and fold my legs out of the car, which isn't the easiest thing to do.

When Rome races back to the car, an orderly follows behind with a wheelchair.

Everything in me tightens up, and I debate slamming the door in the orderly's face. "No! I won't touch that!"

Declan understands my refusal, but Rome reads my hesitation as denial. My boyfriend throws the backdoor open wider and reaches his unsteady hand inside. "The baby is coming, tré-sur."

"No! I'm not going in that. I can walk." Though, the speed at which I can get anywhere might not be up to par.

Declan takes my other hand, helping Rome extract me from the car. "She won't touch a wheelchair, Rome. It's fine. The contractions are six minutes apart. We have time to get her inside."

Rome's eyes close as he no doubt mentally kicks himself for not recalling a little-known fact about my past.

I spent a good portion of my teen years in a wheelchair, hidden away from public view. I lived with my nurse full-time, who took care of me when I could not walk or bathe myself.

I will not go backward. I worked too hard to get on my feet again.

Rome frets at my slow pace as we make our way toward the hospital's entrance. "It would be faster if we used the..."

My growl comes out far more aggressively than I usually permit. "I would sooner give birth in the middle of the sidewalk than get back into that thing. Never, you hear me? Never put me in one of those, no matter how feeble I get."

Rome would promise me the moon right now if I asked him, so he nods and focuses on moving me slowly into the hospital.

Orlando pulls up behind our car. Nico drags his body out of the passenger's side window and sits on the ledge to call out to us. "Um, use the wheelchair, dummies! Get her inside now! The reporters aren't far behind. Paulo and Liesl are dealing with them as best they can."

I turn my head over my shoulder, readying to give Nico a piece of my mind. "Shut up, you..." But that's when a contraction overtakes me, cutting my insult short.

I double over, pausing our progression so I can howl through the pain that I know will only get worse.

It's good that I can feel it. That means the baby is coming, which is what the baby is supposed to do.

At least, that's the pep talk I give myself as my belly hardens and shakes me so roughly, I worry I will fall if Declan or Rome releases either of my hands.

The orderly insists I get into the wheelchair, but then backs off when I gather my bearings enough to cast him my most vicious look of death. "Get that thing away from me."

Rome and Declan move me slowly forward, once my contraction passes and I can stand upright again. It's an arduous task, but they manage to get me inside, check me in and aim me toward where the baby magic happens.

Only we aren't taken to the floor where the other moms are located. Part of the governor's plan for my safety was to keep my location separate from the world while I gave birth. So we are escorted to a different wing of the hospital, which feels like a football field away.

One step at a time, we walk toward our destination, pausing for my contractions when they come.

"That's four minutes," Declan says in a forced calm that I know means he is freaking out. "This baby is coming today, Coco."

Orlando and Nico parked the cars for us, but we are moving so slowly that I can hear their rushing footsteps catching up easily.

Orlando's disapproval is clear in his authoritative tone. "Why is she walking? Nico got her a wheelchair. Here."

I glower at Orlando, gearing up to give him the same belligerent speech I gave the others. "I was in a wheelchair for years in Lonmure. I will not get back into one. I worked too hard to stand."

Orlando takes my temper in stride, his mind racing to fix the problem instead of leaving it be. "Fine. Nico, get in the wheelchair."

"What?" But even as he questions Orlando, Nico obeys.

Man, my childhood bestie sure has come a long way.

Orlando takes my hand from Rome and leads me to the wheelchair, which is not occupied by Nico. "You're going to sit down on Nico's lap. You're not in the wheel-chair. See? You're technically sitting on Nico's lap."

Nico throws his head back. "Anyone want to trade places?"

I want to argue this plan, but a contraction hits me harder than I expect. This one takes my breath away. My knees give out through my howl of pain.

I am grateful for the three men who catch me. They lower me onto Nico's lap while I try to breathe through the tail end of the contraction.

Orlando kneels in front of me, getting in my eyeline while sweat beads on my forehead. "You are not in a wheelchair. You're on Nico's lap. I hope you hate sitting on Nico's lap so much that you realize the wheelchair is necessary when you're in labor."

"I hate this!" I growl, gripping the armrests.

Nico lets loose several dramatic grunts. "Oof! What have you been eating?"

"I'm pregnant! There are two of me sitting on your lap."

"Two elephants?"

I gape at Nico as Declan takes the reins and races the wheelchair down the corridor. "I can't believe you just said that! I weigh a normal amount. I'm carrying a baby."

"A baby elephant."

I should be appalled, and part of me is, but I know Nico is teasing me like the jerk he is. "You're an ass," I tell him, a smile quirking the corner of my mouth.

"You're a fat ass."

"You're a jackass!"

Rome doesn't know if we are joking or serious, but he holds my hand all the same as he runs beside the wheelchair.

Nico holds me on his lap as best he can. "Don't fart on me. I hear elephant farts are deadly."

I snicker but then smack one of his hands that are wrapped around my belly. "Don't make me laugh! I'm terrified!"

Nico changes his tune as he rubs my belly. "It's going to be fine, Coco-bear. I'm right here."

"Is that supposed to make me feel better?"

Nico strokes my stomach. "Vampire women have been giving birth in their homes since forever. You've got an actual hospital with doctors and medicine. It's going to be one lousy day, and then you get a toy."

"Do not call my baby a toy."

Nico chuckles into the back of my shoulder. "I meant I'll bring you a toy. Something fun that'll make you smile."

"A big toy?" I ask, sounding childish, sure, but also I crave the distraction of this ridiculous conversation.

"Depends on how cute the baby is."

"Hilarious. I want a good toy, Nico. I'm holding you to that."

Nico trills his fingers down the length of my stomach. "I know you will. An elephant never forgets."

I try to elbow Nico through my snicker, but I'm too big and awkward to do any real damage.

The twist does something that confuses me. It doesn't hurt, but it's a sensation of release I did not control. The bottom of my pelvis twinges, and in the next breath, I know there is no turning back.

Any hope I might have entertained of this being false labor is a thing of the past.

Nico shifts in his seat. "Is that... Did you just pee on me?"

I breathe through gritted teeth. "I think my water just broke!"

Nico howls his disgust. "On me? Gross! If this is your revenge for me beating you up, then we're even, okay? I'm sorry!" He throws his head back. "Faster, Declan! I'm going to lose it if I don't get out of these clothes soon!"

Rome lets out a bleat of fear. "We're not to the doctor yet! Hurry, Declan!"

Declan belts out a string of unexpected laughter. "I didn't think anything would be funny in this situation, but that was amazing. Well done, Coco. Well done, baby."

"I didn't mean to, Nico," I offer sheepishly. "It's not something I can control." I motion to my body. "And for the record, this doesn't make us even. You still owe me several coffee dates."

Nico holds me tighter. "Fine. Big present, it is." He buries his face into the back of my shoulder. "I'm burning these pants."

Declan gets us to the closed-off wing of the hospital that has been prepped only for me. I wonder if this is the same treatment my mother received when she gave birth to us. There is a security guard at the door, who lets us in and then locks the entrance behind us.

Whatever my life before this moment was, I know that very soon, the world will be forever changed.

3

MY BABY

I am greeted by a team of doctors and nurses the moment Declan wheels me into the sealed-off wing meant only for us. The professionals all have "let's do this" expressions schooling their faces. Even though I am a month early, they are scrubbed in and organized, ready to make history.

Declan did a thorough search on every medical professional here, so we know we can trust them not to harm me or my baby. My doctor from Lonmure is to appear by video so he can instruct them, should anything go wrong when things get going.

Nothing can go wrong. Though truly, I know very little about giving birth, other than the books that Rome read to me every night. If something does go wrong, there is precious little I can do to correct the error. I'm not a doctor.

Right now, I feel like a cow meant to push out a calf without regard for dignity or safety.

I hold up my hands when the nurses reach for me. "I don't know what I'm doing!" I feel compelled to announce.

One of the nurses offers a compassionate smile. "That's okay. We do, and your body does. Together, we'll get your baby out of your stomach and into your arms."

I take a deep breath and nod, finally allowing them to help me off Nico's sopping lap.

The dance is seamless, no doubt because they have done this countless times before. My clothes are removed, and my arms threaded through a hospital gown. I am hooked up to machines to monitor myself and the baby.

I don't think I breathe until the doctor gives me a thumb's up. "Everything is stable. It's early, but I'm not worried. The heartbeat is steady, and you are healthier than ever."

Panic climbs up in my throat as confessions spill out of me. "I ate a pint of ice cream last night! That's not healthy! And I ate three helpings of pot roast two nights ago. Three! No, three and a half, because when Orlando didn't finish all of his, I ate the rest while I was loading the dishwasher."

The doctor presses his lips together through his laughter. "I'll be sure to add that to my file in case your baby comes out shaped like a pot roast. That will explain the mystery."

I gasp, for a second worried that might be a true possibility.

Declan covers me with a thin, scratchy blanket. "He's joking. Deep breaths, sis. We made it. It's all downhill from here."

"For you! I'm the one who has to give birth still!"

Declan's neck shrinks. "Right. I'm sure that will be a piece of cake."

At that moment, a contraction hits me so hard that I scream out. Rome's panicked face does nothing to quell my nerves. Even Declan can't seem to school his features enough to cast a smidgen of calm my way.

Nico and Orlando are in the hallway, but when I gather up enough breath for a second scream, the door flings open and Orlando stomps inside. He rolls up his sleeves as if gearing up to go to war.

When the contraction crests, I lean back into the pillow. "It hurts!"

Orlando anchors his bulky body to my bed, squeezing in beside me so that half my body is leaning on his. Orlando's legs kick up and he gets in my face, his nose an inch from mine. "I'm right here. Say it."

"Orlando is here."

"That's right. There's nothing scary at all if I'm around." His arm coils beneath me so he can cradle me in his arms. "I'm your mate, so I'm not leaving your side until this passes."

Though Orlando cannot take the pain of childbirth away from me, the serenity his mere presence brings settles a little of my fear that I will be bad at this.

That I won't live through this.

Though the doctor, two nurses, Declan and Rome can hear us, I whisper as if the two of us are alone. "My mother died giving birth to me. I shouldn't be doing this!"

I can feel several sets of eyes watching us. I know the newcomers to our strange friendship are looking on in curiosity and borderline horror, seeing the formidable Orlando cuddling up to the Last Deadblood.

Orlando kisses the tip of my nose. "Your mother didn't have me as her mate." Then he nuzzles his nose to mine. "Tell me who I am to you."

"You're my mate," I tell him. "You and Rome."

"That's right. What else?"

I peck his lips as sweat rolls down my temple. "You're my friend. You're my guard."

"That's good. What else?"

I snuggle into his arms and shut my eyes, fending off the fear of reality for as long as I am able. "You're my big sweetie pie. You won't let anything bad come for me."

Orlando's arm rubs up and down my arm. "That's right. I'm your big sweetie pie. Everything is going to be fine, Colette my dove."

"Orlando my love," I whisper, my breath shallow. "Stay with me?"

"Always," he promises.

Rome pulls up a chair on Orlando's other side, so my boyfriend can get in my eyeline. His arm stretches across his cousin's torso so he can hold my hand. "The machine says another contraction is coming. Hold tight to us."

I squeeze the living daylights out of Rome's hand when the next wave hits harder than I was expecting. I bury my scream in Orlando's neck until the pain passes.

Having them with me is the balm my soul needs.

They will not let me die. In fact, they will see this labor through to its glorious end, ensuring my baby has the best life any child could ever be granted.

Love pushes out a portion of my fear as the hours tick by, filled with intermittent bouts of screaming and hushed oaths of loyalty.

When the doctor warns me it's time to push, I don't let go of the men I adore.

My mates hold onto me as history opens up, making room for me and my new baby.

4

MIRACLE X

Never in my life have I seen anyone more striking than this incredible child. Even after a twenty-seven-hour labor with plenty of touch and go moments, I will never tire of watching this perfect child.

"I don't understand," Nico admits, which is no different than the tune he was singing half an hour ago when the doctor explained everything to both families. Of course, that was largely in medical jargon which I barely understood, and I've known about this twist of nature since the second ultrasound.

Rome casts a look of silent pleading to Declan to field this one. He hasn't left my side this entire time, for which I am grateful.

"Intersex," Declan explains, "is when a baby is born with born sex organs. The baby is both male and female."

Nico's nose squinches. "So the baby has a..." He takes a

deep breath as he motions to his crotch like a caveman. "And a..."

I nod, wondering how this is so hard for him to grasp. "Yes. The internal sex organs might also be both, or more predominantly one. Either way, the baby's gender is X, meaning intersex." My voice is scratchy from all the screaming.

I'm just grateful to have had a shower and an hour's nap since the whole ordeal.

Actually, I'm told I passed out from the blood loss, but I got a nap out of the deal, so I'm not complaining. And Declan was there to make sure my blood was properly disposed of, so it cannot be weaponized.

Nico pinches the bridge of his nose. "I don't know what to do with that information. So what about her blood? His blood? How do I even say it?" He throws up his hands, exasperated. "Is the blood deadly?"

I cast Nico a bland smile as I cradle the most perfect baby to my chest. The IV tube in my hand is cumbersome, and my hospital gown keeps falling off my shoulder, but no annoyance can keep me from cradling my love. "The baby is going to be X gender until they are old enough to choose what they would like, if anything."

Nico shoots me a dubious look. "Hello, the kid can't choose nothing. It's one or the other."

I bite my tongue to keep from cussing at Nico in front of the baby. "Rome? Educate your brother. I don't want to swear."

Rome leans in from his rocking chair beside my hospital bed, looking very much like an experienced father as he gazes lovingly at the two of us. "Nonbinary means a person chooses neither gender or both genders. Whatever the baby chooses is fine: boy, girl, neither or both."

Orlando stands in the doorway still. He hasn't let himself come all the way inside since I came to in a far less chaotic world. It is no surprise to me that my big sweetie pie is fearless of vicious bad guys, but wary of a tiny baby. His arms tuck behind his back. "But is the baby's blood lethal? Are you the Last Deadblood or is the baby?"

My jaw tightens. "Unless either of you would like to volunteer to test it, I plan on never finding out. It's actually not standard practice to take a baby's blood and use it to coat bullets to see if the blood is lethal."

Nico sighs. "So I can't say 'he' or 'she'? What do I say?"

"They," I respond succinctly.

"That's impossible. I'll never get that right. Hey, they want to go to the park. Can I take them?" Nico's face sours. "That's weird."

"You'll adjust. I had to learn to stop calling you 'that asshole' and start calling you 'Nico'. It was an adjustment, but because I'm *not* an asshole, I did it. Easy-peasy."

Nico mimes a laugh at my jab. "Seriously, though. This isn't going to go over well."

A rage the likes of which hasn't risen in me in quite some time roils in my chest.

When I open my mouth, my voice is darker, lower and

with plenty of force behind my words. "My baby is perfect. I don't care what people think of them. They are welcome in this world, and you, their uncle, will see to it. You will be this baby's greatest advocate. If the world doesn't have room for my baby, then it doesn't have room for anyone who gets in my way over this." I thumb my baby's cherubic cheek, my voice returning to a delicate coo. "Because you're the most amazing baby that ever was, aren't you. You're a miracle. If they don't know what to call you, that's what they'll say. 'The Miracle', not 'the boy' or 'the girl'."

Orlando's eyes are wide. "That was terrifying. Is that what it's like to be a mother? Someone crosses your kid even hypothetically, and you turn into a demon on a mission?"

I blink up at him with my most angelic expression. "Yes. Is that a problem?"

Orlando blanches. "No, Ma'am. What can I get you? Anything? Ice chips? I was good at fetching those while you were in labor."

I shake my head. "I can drink regular water now, but thank you." I don't want to push Orlando to come closer if he's not ready, but part of me feels incomplete without being able to share this moment with my other mate.

Orlando stayed with me in the delivery room, which wasn't part of the plan. I can still hear him barking at the doctor every time I screamed. "She needs your human medicine! Give her more medicine!"

When I passed the point of being able to have

anything to dull the pain, Orlando lost his mind. He even went so far as tearing open his wrist with his fang to feed me drops of his blood in case that would do something.

"Are you sure you don't want to hold them?" I ask Orlando, snuggling my baby closer.

Orlando shakes his head, still pale from watching a woman give birth and being able to do nothing to help the situation.

"Rome hasn't eaten in a while. Nico, could you grab him something to eat?"

Nico stands. "Sure thing." Instead of moving toward the exit, he migrates to my side, bowing his head to kiss the baby's forehead. "I'll be right back, little Miracle. Your Uncle Nico loves you." As if my heart couldn't melt any further, Nico then does something none of us expect. He leans over and kisses my forehead. "You did it, Sis. You did the impossible. Whatever an X gender is, I can get on board. Miracle is amazing." He lowers his chin. "Does this get me out of diaper duty?"

I snort at his joke that isn't really a joke. "You were never going to be on diaper duty, dumbass."

He scoffs at my insult, as if he cannot believe anyone would call him that. "Did you hear that, Miracle? Your mother just called your favorite person in the world a dumbass. I think every time your mommy insults me, I'm going to buy you a present that's too big to fit inside your bedroom."

The two of us share a smirk before he leaves to scrounge up food for Rome.

Declan chuckles to himself. "My, how times have changed. That baby really is a miracle worker. Nico turned over a new leaf this past year. I never would have guessed crap like that could come out of his surly mug. Good for him." He leans toward me. "But obviously I'm the favorite uncle. Let's be real."

"Obviously." I glance at Orlando. "Any word on getting Senator Washburn booted out of office? How's that going?"

Orlando opens his mouth to answer, but Rome's rebuttal is firm. "No. None of that exists inside this hospital room. We've got security blocking off the entire wing, so we don't have to worry about anyone stealing your blood or taking pictures of our miracle. Nothing like that is happening today. The governor will take care of the mayhem, and the people will demand justice takes place. We've done all we can and should do, so we're finished. You just gave birth this morning. You're going to take a real maternity leave."

I want to protest, but as I am currently cuddling my little miracle, I'm not sure my words will hold water.

Declan and Rome talk quietly about the crib, which has been set up for months, but needs fresh sheets, because... God forbid we use the sheets that have been on the little mattress for two months.

I cannot comprehend how much I love this child. The cherubic cheeks and button nose are mine, but the full lips and angular chin are Rome's. Miracle is the perfect blend of us both. Rome's blue eyes stare at me through the face of my baby, watching me as if I matter.

And we do. We matter to each other.

Declan's voice quiets. "What are you thinking about?"

I clear my throat, worried I might burst into tears. "I wonder if this is how Mom felt when she held us for the first time. Then I wonder if Mom ever got to hold me." I shake my head. "My heart is so full, it actually hurts. I didn't know I could love someone so instantly and wholly."

Declan smiles at the two of us. "I think you've got this mom thing down. Day one on the job, and you're already knocking it out of the park."

Insecurity brings a slight tremble to my voice. "Don't let me screw this up?"

Declan shakes his head. "Never."

Footsteps echo toward us at too fast a pace to be calm. My spine stiffens, but Rome is out of his rocking chair and standing in front of my bed before the person comes into view.

Declan does the same while Orlando moves into the hallway, speaking in hushed tones with the person in question.

"Nothing's wrong. It's all fine," I tell everyone, including my miracle.

Including myself.

But when Orlando comes into the room, his tight

expression tells me how very wrong I am. His voice is quiet and controlled. "There's been a breach. We have to move."

My heart pounds as I clutch Miracle to my chest.

I thought we had more time before the world would come for us, telling us we don't belong.

I need more time.

5

REVOLUTIONARIES IN THE HOSPITAL

$\mathcal{I}$ am sure the wheelchair has never been raced down the hallway before, but to its credit, it doesn't seem to mind the exercise. I, on the other hand, am winded from the simple task of being upright. After labor that intense and only being given two hours of reprieve, I am in no shape for even sitting upright. My stomach muscles are all scattershot, unsure how to make my torso sit up straight.

I didn't fight them on getting into the wheelchair. I'm not sure I can stand yet. There's no way I can make a quick escape. The things I fought against so ardently yesterday are a mere echo of convenience now. I have my baby to think about. I can't worry about my PTSD.

Rome has Miracle, and even though I can see our baby is safe in his capable arms, tears stream down my cheeks. I know I am being irrational. The most important thing is for us to escape without incident. But Miracle is too far away. I need my baby in my arms. I need to hold them to my chest. My breasts feel naked without my baby resting over them.

I have to get a grip.

But I can't, so I sob into my hand while Declan races us down the hallway and into the elevator. "This is a mistake," Orlando frets when the doors close us in. "It's announcing to the attackers which floor we're going to." He shakes his head and presses the button for the doors to open. "We'll take the stairs."

"I can't!" I wail, scared and beyond my breaking point. "I just gave birth! I can't even walk yet."

Declan wheels me toward the stairwell all the same, stopping only when we get to the top step.

Orlando gets down on one knee in front of me while Rome races down the steps with Paulo at his side and Miracle in his arms. "I'm going to carry you, okay?"

"You can't! I just gave birth!"

Orlando takes both of my hands in his and kisses them. "It's the only way. Don't I always keep you safe?"

I nod, but I don't want to give him that. Whoever is behind this is horrible. "If this is Fintan, put me down and shoot a bullet in his brain. Understood?"

"That's my girl." Orlando is as careful as he can be with me while Declan takes out his gun to give us proper cover. Liesl takes the rear, weapon drawn.

Though Orlando is careful with my body, there is no

part of me that does not feel bruised. I bite down on my lower lip to keep from crying out as I am lightly jostled in his arms.

The most acute pain of all is the fact that Miracle is out of my eyeline. Rome's footsteps are still descending, but my baby is too far away. My insides leap with panic I cannot control as hormones flood me with a maternal protectiveness. I am equal parts loving and vicious.

My arms don't have enough strength in them at the moment to cling to Orlando, so I trust him to not drop me as he flies down flight after flight, making his way to the back exit of the hospital, where our cars are stashed.

Liesl talks to her team on her phone as we race to the bottom of the steps, but nothing that she says gives me any hope that the situation is under control.

I sob into Orlando's collar, my heart breaking because this isn't how it was supposed to be.

Or maybe this was always how this was going to go. Maybe the world isn't capable of giving us any other option.

It's a heartbreak from which I am not sure I will ever heal.

Orlando's foot stumbles only once, but he doesn't drop me. He clings tight to me, even as we step out onto the main floor to the tune of men shouting and civilians screaming.

I close my eyes and clutch Orlando around the neck as the first bullet is fired.

I don't want to see the glass atrium, nor the people who came in for medical help squatting behind plants and under chairs. I don't want to make out the ski-masked shapes of the men who want nothing more than the money that might come to them if they are successful in stealing my blood.

All I want is my baby.

"Hand over the Last Deadblood!" a man shouts in the beats between shots taken.

I scream into Orlando's shirt, terrified of anything happening to my miracle. All the people I love are here, and there is precious little chance no one will be hurt in the process.

I don't have my gun. I can't protect my baby. I can't defend the men I love.

Orlando is a target, because he is carrying me. Can he even wield his weapon properly? Can Rome?

Declan cries out as he fires his weapon. I don't see anything because my face is buried in Orlando's shirt. Even if I wasn't hiding my face like a child, I wouldn't be able to see through my curtain of tears anyway.

The baby's ears. They are too precious and delicate to be around gunfire. Miracle is two hours old.

Baby's first gunfight.

Liesl calls out commands and Declan falls in line, from what I can make out. She directs him where to fire, and my brother takes the shots alongside her while I sob into Orlando's shirt.

I can see the back of Rome's head, which means he is alive and has our miracle. They have to get to safety, no matter what. With everything in me, I will speed to reach Rome's feet, so he can get Miracle away from this madness.

Another shot, and Orlando trips, losing his step.

My scream traps itself behind my closed teeth as I am jostled, my body lurching forward haphazardly.

Orlando growls through a pain that I can only hope isn't lethal. He hoists me up while his left leg goes out from under him.

It is the gentlest I have ever been dropped. Even as my body lands on the hard floor, Orlando holds tight to me so I don't crash down on anything but the cushion of his arms.

I cry out from equal parts panic and the pain of being dropped. "Orlando, no!" Fear floods me while I do my best to cover his torso with mine. I crawl over his body to shield it from any bullets that might prove lethal to my mate.

Orlando's teeth grind while he tries to muscle through the pain and stay focused. "Declan!" Orlando calls to my brother, his voice breaking.

Declan stoops down and scoops me to my feet. His weapon isn't being fired while he helps Orlando up, winding my mate's arm around his shoulders so the two can amble forward together. Liesl covers us while we make our slow escape. She trails behind so she can stand between me and any fire aimed my way.

Little does Liesl understand that the fire is never aimed

at me. It's the abductions I need to worry about, not the bullets.

Orlando is still moving, so I know he wasn't shot with a lethal bullet. Though, why the revolutionaries wouldn't use bullets dipped in my blood is a mystery to me.

My vision scans the room for people I might recognize, namely my brother. Though for the most part, the revolutionaries are wearing ski masks, there is one who discarded his for reasons I can only guess.

"Lampert," I breathe, waddling as much as I am running. My father's former sheriff's deputy races after us. His pudgy face stares at me from across the hospital's foyer. He is in his police uniform, no doubt not expecting to have to show his true colors today.

Officer Lampert wasn't arrested for his part in helping Fintan escape. They couldn't pin the crime on him without it slipping off his slimy demeanor. But now there are witnesses cowering under chairs, watching a police officer aim his weapon at their Madam Deadblood.

Receptionists, nurses and patients are on the floor, their hands over their heads because that is what they have been ordered to do by the angry men with guns. People cry out when they realize targets have been verified, and their Deadblood is fleeing for her life.

The revolutionaries were expecting us to come down the elevator, so more are still rushing toward us as we amble to the back exit.

Rome is already out the door, hopefully running

toward the car and finding a safe escape. Miracle is in his arms, which is just about the safest place one could be.

Liesl screams when Lampert fires. He hits her in the shoulder and knocks her into me. I pull away from Declan's side and grip Liesl's good arm as best I can. It is an effort to force her body to remain upright, but I am not going to let go of the guard in charge of keeping me alive. I drag Liesl with me, her feet stumbling in time with Orlando's janky gait just ahead of us.

My body hurts. It just went through the trauma of childbirth, yet here I am, ambling while tears stream down my cheeks.

I hear the cocking of a shotgun—a vastly different sound than the other weapons. My speed picks up as best it can while Liesl shoots as well as she can manage to give us a clear path of escape. I tug her toward the only exit that isn't blocked by the revolutionaries.

It's not until I reach the exit that I realize I am not escaping.

I am being herded.

My bare feet skid to a stop. "Declan, no! They're waiting for us out there!"

Declan turns, but it's only just in time to see what happens after the shotgun fires.

It's not a bullet that hits me square in the back. A beanbag round socks me in the spine, knocking me forward off my feet and launching me onto my face.

It's a scream I didn't realize I was still capable of

making. My throat is raw from all the screaming I did while pushing out Miracle.

The pain of being knocked on my freshly deflated stomach is more than my bruised body can take.

I don't know whose hands grip my arms. I don't know where they are taking me. All I know is that I cannot think beyond the pain of the moment.

I can only hope Miracle and Rome have escaped.

6

ABDUCTED

I awake in the backseat of a sedan, where I have been shoved unceremoniously across the seat. My head is bent at an odd angle. My back is twisted and my legs are splayed unnaturally.

I dare not move. I dare not speak. I don't know if I am capable of doing either of those things. I open my eyes only for the span of a blink, taking in the gray interior of a sedan I do not recognize and therefore do not trust.

A voice I recognize as Officer Lampert growls from the driver's seat. "How is it you couldn't kidnap a baby? A baby, Fintan. Honestly. If your heart isn't in this, bow out already. You had a clear, open shot. You could have taken Rome out. You could have taken the baby."

My eldest brother's voice crackles through the car's Bluetooth, breaking my heart. I haven't heard Fintan's voice since he murdered our father eight months ago.

"Lampert, you act like the Valentinos are sitting ducks. They're deadly killers, who are well armed. Vampires are dangerous, or have you forgotten that little fact?"

"Excuses," Lampert replies.

"Is my sister alive?"

"She's breathing. I'll be to you in twenty. We needed that baby, Fintan." Officer Lampert is the only other person in the car, which means I am in this on my own.

Every part of my body screams for relief, for a pain killer, but I know that where I am going there will be no reprieve from the agony.

I have a small window where I can fight for my freedom, if I can lift my hands to fight at all.

I can do this. I have to do this.

The question is how.

My head turns slightly to the side, where I am sure Lampert cannot see my face in the rearview mirror.

Maybe I could strangle Lampert with his seatbelt. That's possible, or maybe it would be if I was strong, which I am not. I bled a lot while giving birth. I am supposed to be on bedrest, like a normal woman, not wrestling a cop in a fight to the death.

It's then that my gaze touches on the silver glint of the steel running through the butt of his gun in its holster on Lampert's hip.

I cannot reach it without giving away the fact that I am awake and alert. I can't move all that quickly, and I'm not positive of my dexterity. My heart screams in silence for my baby, but I keep myself focused as best I can. I need to rely on at least some parts of my body to enact a decent attempt at an escape.

We aren't on the freeway, judging by the speed limit and frequent prolonged stops. Lampert is taking the back roads, most likely to keep his car off the radar in case it has been reported.

I cannot simply wait for the cops to find me. For one, I don't know if they are quality heroes in blue. And two, they might never find me, or if they do, how much of my blood will have been harvested to make lethal weapons before they track me down?

We hit a patch of uneven road, and I know this is my only chance.

I keep my reach careful at first, making sure my arm stays low and out of obvious sight. But when we hit a particularly rough bit of gravel, my hand darts out and snatches at Lampert's gun.

It doesn't yank free easily, even after I unlatch the weapon from its holster. Lampert jerks the car when he realizes I am awake and far more ready to defend myself than either of us could have guessed.

It is all the effort I have to sit up, but I manage the feat with the force of sheer will.

Blame it on my mate's blood. Blame it on maternal adrenaline and the need to get to my baby. Blame it on cold, hard revenge.

Lampert doesn't get out a single sentence before the gun fires, sinking a bullet straight through his temple.

I am done with this man, and now, so is the world.

The car jerks because I didn't think it through. Fintan's voice calls through the car, asking what Lampert just fired at.

The call disconnects when the car crashes into a telephone poll, launching me forward to bruise my body impossibly more.

7

HITCHHIKING HOME

I will escape. I will find my baby. I don't care that I have bits of glass peppering my face and arms. It doesn't matter that my ears are still ringing from the explosion of the bullet leaving its chamber to find its new home in Officer Lampert's skull.

I have to find my Miracle.

I am barefoot and in a bloody hospital gown, but as it turns out, that is the perfect power outfit when you're trying to flag down some good, honest help on the side of the road. I limp, searching for a vehicle that can take me to safety.

The autumn wind whistles through the thin material that whips around my knees. The gown is wet with blood —both mine and Officer Lampert's, so I am that much colder. My body shivers, whether from the chill in the air, a need for my medication, or from the trauma, I cannot tell.

Maybe I am in shock.

Took me long enough.

The first car that sees me in the evening light skids to a stop. A woman rolls down her window, her mouth agape. "What the... Let me call an ambulance."

"Not yet. I need a ride. Please. Take me away from here." When the woman behind the wheel looks wary, I explain my plight. "I'm Colette Kennedy. I am the Deadblood, and that man in there was trying to take my blood so he can kill vampires. He abducted me and I escaped. Please, I need to get away from him!"

The woman looks to be in her forties, her eyes widening with shock. "Yes! Yes, of course. Get in quick. Let's get you out of here. Where can I take you, Madam Deadblood?" She dips her freckled face. "Your Majesty?"

"Thank you." It's all I can do to get into the car. It's my last bit of adrenaline. Once I sit in the seat, all energy deserts me. Even my voice sounds weak. "To Mayfield, please. The West End. The Valentino mansion."

The woman gulps audibly, but to her credit, she grips the steering wheel and drives in the direction of the West End. "Wouldn't you prefer I take you to a hospital?"

I shake my head, though even that small motion pains me. "Not safe. That's where I was abducted from. My brother can help me. He's a medic. He's... Can I borrow your phone?" My chest heaves unevenly as my body screams at me that I need something for the pain.

The woman fumbles with her purse while she drives

and then hands me her phone, her eyes on the road ahead. "Of course. I'm Amber. I'll take you wherever you need to go, Madam Deadblood. But I have to be honest, you need medical attention, like, now. Do you promise your brother can actually help you, because I don't want to drive the Deadblood to her death. I believe in your mission."

I swallow hard, knowing I must look every bit as ghastly as I feel. "My brother can help me, I promise. Thank you."

Amber's car picks up speed, driving us away from the scene of the multiple crimes. "Anything you need. Anything. I have a friend who's a vampire. What you're doing is... I'm listening. Whatever you're saying, I'm listening. I voted to help instate vampire voting rights. I marched for the cause just two months ago."

Amber keeps going, telling me all the ways she is supportive. Every sentence she says calms me a small amount, letting me know that I haven't gone from one abduction to another.

I press the digits for my brother's cell phone number. The pain echoing through my body tightens my tone. "Declan?" I'm frightened, worried they didn't all make it out. If anything happened to the people I love...

"Coco? Is that you? Oh! Colette! Where are you? Lampert, that snake! Did you escape? I'll come for you! Where did he take you?"

I can hear Rome barking in the background for my brother to hand the phone to him.

My abdomen aches so badly that just talking is an effort. I didn't realize sitting upright requires muscular control, which is a necessity I do not have in large supply. "I'm just leaving the intersection of Maple and Klein. I got away from him. Someone is driving me to the Valentino mansion. Is that place still safe?"

There are precious few safe places anymore, but vampire territory is usually too scary for most humans to traipse through. Plus, a human stands out, so if they are intending on being sneaky, that's not the place to do it.

Declan heaves a sigh of relief. "Yes, that's perfect. Don't stop on the way. Straight here, Coco. I've got the guys here now. Tell me what Lampert did to you. What should I prepare for?"

"I need my pills!" I cry. "I need my baby! I just gave birth. Where is Miracle? Are they safe?"

Declan's calm is juxtaposed by Rome's cry of rage that sounds mingled with agony, matching my own heartbreak. "Give me my wife, Declan!"

Declan rushes his reply. "They're all alive and in the mansion. Here, Rome. My gosh."

The voice switches from a concerned brother to a frightened Rome. "Where are you? I can come to you."

"I'm on my way to you. No more than an hour, and we should be there."

Amber nods and steps on the gas.

My hand moves to my stomach, which feels disjointed

and scarred. "Rome, tell me you and Miracle are safe. Tell me our baby is okay."

"They're perfect," Rome assures me, quelling the hammering of my heart. "The second we got home, Declan went to work making sure we're all going to live through this. The bullet is out of Orlando's leg, and Liesl is on her way to recovery. Nothing happened to Miracle at all. Just a little gunfire that scared them a bit. I'll have a doctor check their hearing to make sure there was no damage. But they know my voice, tré-sur. Our baby knows my voice. When I'm near, they get this little breath that I know means they recognize me. See? All those times I spent reading to your belly paid off."

I laugh through hysterical tears, nodding while I let his words wash over me. "You're safe. You're all safe?"

"All we're missing is you. Come home to us, my little cannoli."

I sob into the phone, unable to exercise any semblance of control over my emotions. "I'm on my way."

Rome doesn't let me off the phone, even when I grunt through the pain that echoes through my body. "Can you tell me how you escaped? Can you tell me if you're injured? Any information would be helpful so Declan can be all set up for you when you get here."

"Orlando's okay?" I ask, ignoring Rome's question for the moment. I have to know my mates are whole and well.

"He's angry at himself. He won't calm down until he sees you. He says it's all his fault because he dropped you."

I let out a joyless snort. "Um, he only dropped me because he was shot. Did he forget that little detail?"

"You know Orlando." Rome's tone deepens. "Tell me what happened."

"Officer Jaren Lampert happened," I respond flatly. "I woke up in the backseat of his car. He didn't know I was awake, so I waited for a bumpy road and yanked his gun from his belt."

I swallow hard as I cast Amber a look of apology. She is already gaunt without having to hear the gory details of my escape.

I wait until Rome's cussing crests. "He was talking with Fintan on the phone in the car."

Rome snarls into the phone. "That snake."

"Fintan was concerned about me," I say quietly through my tears. "Wanted to make sure I was still alive."

Rome's tone takes on that of a teacher. "That's because you are no good to Fintan if you are dead. He wants you for your blood. He doesn't want you to live because he loves you. Never forget that."

My eyes close as more tears slide down my face. "Let me pretend my brother loves me. I gave birth today, Rome. Let me pretend."

Rome softens. "Of course. I'm sorry. Yes, Fintan loves you. He wants you alive because he cares about you."

I know the lie is hard for Rome to muster, but I need to hear it all the same. He produces the fabrication that shreds at his moral fiber without hesitation, simply because that is the balm my soul requires.

Amber reaches over and holds my free hand. I don't realize how badly my tremors are acting up until she has a hard time gripping my slick fingers because they are so jumpy.

I burst into fresh tears at the display of basic kindness once our hands connect. I need to not be alone in my agony right now. The pain in my body is so acute that only the breaking of my heart can overshadow it.

"I shot Officer Lampert in the head," I admit in broken sobs as the gory visual replays in my mind. "I shot him, Rome. He won't be coming for me ever again."

There is not a hint of condemnation in Rome's reply. "Good. That's good, little cannoli. I know that must have been hard. You did the right thing. Miracle needs their mom. You're on your way home to us?"

"Yes. A good Samaritan picked me up on the side of the road. Her car needs to be detailed, Rome. My blood is all over it."

"How much blood?"

I glance down, realizing that I bled through the postpartum pads a long time ago. "A lot," I whisper.

The woman glances at my legs and gasps. "It's okay," she promises me. "We'll get you to a doctor."

"My brother can help me," I tell her. "Keep on the course to the West End."

"Let me talk to the driver," Rome insists.

I hand over the phone apologetically, but the woman doesn't falter. Her spine straightens, as if she has been waiting her whole life to serve the cause, and finally her day has come. "Hello, Mister Valentino. I'm Amber Bantan. I voted for vampire voting rights and marched two months ago for the cause. I have a friend who is a vampire, and I'm ready to help however I can."

I can hear Rome's chuckle at Amber's nervous rambling. "That's good," I hear him say. "One thing that needs to happen is we have to take your car when you get here so we can get rid of any traces of Colette's blood. The good news is your car will look better than new. The bad news is you'll have to wait while it gets detailed, so your plans for the day might be thrown off by an hour or so."

Amber nods, her red hair swishing over her shoulder. "Of course. Anything you need. She, um, Madam Dead-blood won't let me take her to a hospital, but I'm pretty sure she needs one. Did she really just give birth?"

Rome talks Amber through the basics of the events of the day. By the time he finishes, the only color on Amber's face is the brown of her freckles.

Amber grimaces as she glances at me. "The car she escaped from was in bad shape. Mister Valentino, Madam Deadblood has bits of glass on her face and arms. She... It's not great."

"She shot him while the car was moving?"

"It looks to be that way. And for what it's worth, I had a baby last year. She needs something with codeine every six hours and ibuprofen every six hours, alternating so she's taking one of those two things every three hours. The pain will be... Can you get your hands on something like that by the time we get there, or should I stop off and try to pick something up? She's shaking, Mister Valentino."

Rome's voice is firm. "No, I'll send someone to pick up her meds. Drive right to my home in the West End and don't stop for anything. If a cop tries to pull you over, don't stop. Understood? Don't stop until you get here. The man my wife shot is a cop. We don't know who we can trust."

"You can trust me," Amber vows, her chest puffed. "I will bring Madam Deadblood to you, Sir. You have my word."

I can hear Rome trying to hide the amusement in his tone over her soldier-like compliance. "Very good. Thank you, Miss Bantan. Your help will not go unrewarded."

Amber shakes her head. "My reward is being able to sleep at night, knowing I was able to help."

I can't smile at her because the pain is too great. I lean my seat back and grip the door, bracing myself because even though I have escaped, the aftermath is far from over.

Amber's volume drops, but it's not like I can't hear her, even though I can tell that is what she is trying to accomplish. "She lost a lot of blood. I'm worried we won't make it to you in time."

I hear Rome barking to Declan, telling him what I will need when I arrive.

"Keep me on the phone," Rome insists. "I want Colette

to be able to hear our baby, in case Miracle makes any cooing noises. They don't want to be apart. Maybe hearing each other on the phone will help."

Grief spills over me as my uterus lurches. I need my baby. I have to get back to my loves.

Amber keeps on the road ahead, taking me to the home I never want to be without.

I can only hope I reach them before it is too late.

8

DECLAN'S BOYFRIEND

The codeine is doing nothing to numb the pain of having dozens of shards of glass tweezed from my arms and face. Though Declan is careful, Rome hit his limit twenty minutes ago.

Declan's jaw is tight, but he keeps his eyes on the work at hand. "You know, you don't have to be in the room for this, Rome. You can go check on Orlando, or you know, just plain go away."

Rome's face is gaunt, his eyes rounded with a mania he doesn't often give voice to. "You know I can't do that. I need to be here."

"You are going to smother her," Declan sings. My brother sometimes sings his words when he is stressed, so I know he is more worried than his focused features let on.

But Rome and I know there is no such thing as him being

able to love me too much. We have lived too dangerous of lives to be worried about things like needing space. We need safety. We need what little comfort this world has granted us.

We need each other, and both of us need this baby.

It is an act of true courage and torture to be near Miracle and not hold them. But being that I have glass still peppering my body, holding my infant is not the safest option at the moment.

"You have to stop crying," Declan scolds me. "Your tears are making this piece too slick to grab."

"I'm sorry!" I snap. "You try having a baby ripped out of your vagina, then go straight into a gunfight, then be abducted and taken away from your baby. Then shoot a man in the head, get in a car crash, and find your way to safety all in the same day. Let's see how cool and calm you are then!"

Declan holds my gaze and takes a deep breath, miming for me to do the same. "Be as upset as you like, but if you want to hold Miracle, then you'll let me work as quick as I can, which means no more tears for like, five whole minutes."

My lower lip quivers. "You know I can't do that."

Lucas comes into the guest bedroom on the first floor, where I have been lain. "Did someone order a cup of Orlando's special tea?"

I nod greedily, which only makes Declan huff. "You have to keep your head still."

"Please," I beg. "I need something more than the medicine. It's not doing what it's supposed to."

Rome snorts, though there is no joy in the sound. "I'm not sure enough medicine exists to numb what your body has been through."

Lucas presses the teacup to my lips because my hands are too shaky to hold anything without dropping it.

That's another reason why I can't hold Miracle yet.

I sip the warm liquid, grateful Orlando thought to give me a dose of his blood, in case that grants me even a hiccup of relief. "Thank you. Tell Orlando thank you."

Lucas speaks to me, but he glances at Rome. "Orlando isn't going to stay in the living room much longer. He keeps trying to get off the couch and come in here."

Rome shakes his head. "Do what you can to get him to calm down. She has to stop bleeding before any vampire can go near her. I know my cousin; he won't be able to be in the room without holding her when she is this distressed."

Lucas nods. "Agreed. Just warning you that I have moral qualms about wrestling a man who was just shot in the leg."

"Fair enough." Rome's eyes light up. "Give him a job that will help her. Ask him to make her a meal."

I blanch. "I can't eat. I feel sick to my stomach, Rome."

Rome tilts his head at me. "Eventually you have to eat something. It's been a while since you've had more than ice chips."

That's true, but the pain is the only thing in my mind, so hunger takes a backseat.

Lucas nods. "On it. Good idea. I'll help him, because he's not exactly sturdy on his feet. But that's better than him coming in here prematurely. Besides, I think all of us could use something to eat."

Declan frowns at the men. "Orlando should be sitting down. He was shot in the leg."

Rome blows a raspberry while he cradles Miracle to his cheek. "He'll heal just fine. The pain will keep him centered, so he doesn't come in here and get too near Coletta's blood."

Declan shakes his head at the logic. "Whatever."

Once I've drained my cup, Lucas kisses my forehead and exits to deal with Orlando.

I fix my eyes on my brother. "He's not bad, your guy."

Declan's mouth tightens. "Lucas is not my guy anymore."

That's just about the only thing that can distract me from the discomfort of having glass plucked from my skin with tweezers. "What?"

Declan gives me a slight shake of his head. "It's fine. I don't want to talk about it."

My sadness turns to unvarnished anger. "I don't give a crap what you want to talk about, Declan. What did you do? Why did you end things with that sweet man?"

Declan challenges me with his glare. "What makes you think I ended things?" When his protest is met with my look of disbelief, his shoulders fall. "Oh, fine. It was me. I had to. You know how our life is."

My nose crinkles. "What is that supposed to mean?"

Declan's face is inches from mine as he pulls a piece of glass from the side of my nose. "It means look at our life. You had a baby, and you were abducted the same day."

"What does that have to do with Lucas?"

"I love Lucas. I can't have him caught up in all of this. It's selfish of me to want to keep him close. So I ended things. I don't want this life for him. I'm in it, but he can walk away and have a good life."

My mouth falls open. "Are you insane?"

Rome moves to the hallway and calls for Lucas to come back inside. Once Lucas enters, I notice the downward tilt of his head, the submissive demeanor that says he will still be here for us whether or not Declan's head is firmly lodged up his own ass.

Rome takes control of the situation, now that Lucas is witness to his words. "Declan, do you think I signed up to be with your sister because I wanted an easy life?"

Declan snorts. "No."

"I love your sister, so all the obstacles are small in comparison to the horror of living without her. If she did to me what you did to Lucas—breaking things off with me in order to protect me—that would be a whole new kind of agony."

I shake my head at my brother. "I know you think you're doing the right thing, but you can't go making decisions like that for someone else. Lucas has a right to decide how much danger he is willing to risk for you."

"All of it," Lucas rules without needing a moment to catch up. "There is nothing I wouldn't give up to be with you, Declan."

For the first time, I see Declan's unaffected demeanor melt to insecurity. "Don't you think I know that? I can't do it, Lucas. If anything happened to you, I couldn't survive it. This way is best. Now I know that even if I can't be with you, you're out there living and smiling and laughing. The world still gets to have you." He motions around the room. "This life isn't meant for us to survive it. We are in it, but you have a chance to get out. So yeah, I'm making that choice for you because I won't survive it if you die in this mess. I'm not strong enough to watch the light fade from your eyes."

Lucas stares Declan down. "Don't you see that you've already stolen the light from my eyes? The second you ended things, there was no joy worth considering." Lucas crosses the room and cups Declan's weary face. "Don't you understand that there is no life for me out there unless you're in it? I would gladly walk through this Hell if it means I get to hold your hand."

Declan's heartbreak fills the room while Miracle squawks. "But I love you too much to let you! And I'm not strong enough for this. I can't keep going if this life takes you. I already lost my father. I lost my mother. My brother is lost to us all. And today, I nearly lost my sister.

One of us has to make it out of this alive. I need it to be you."

Lucas takes the tweezers and antiseptic out of Declan's hands and pulls him to his feet. Lucas wraps his arms around my brother's frame, and within seconds, Declan falls apart in Lucas' embrace.

"I can't do this!" Declan admits. "I thought I was doing the right thing, pushing you away, but I'm dead inside. Completely lost without you."

Lucas' brown fingers tangle in the hair in the back of my brother's head. Their cheeks press together as Lucas makes it his business to be gentle with my brother when he is all turned around and making bad decisions. "Shh. You don't have to worry about that. I'm here, aren't I? Just because you broke up with me doesn't mean I want out. You can't make me walk away from your sister when she needs help. Breaking up with you doesn't do anything but force you to go through this alone. Good idea or bad idea?"

I love the sweet way they are with each other.

"Bad idea," Declan admits through a sniffle that doesn't possess an ounce of pride. "I'm sorry, Lucas! I just..."

But Lucas doesn't need the apology. He holds my brother tighter and kisses his cheek. "It never happened. It was a tiny bad patch we will never have to go through again. I'm in this, understood? The only reason you end things is because you don't love me anymore. You don't push me away to protect me. I am safest when I'm with you."

Declan's chest expands as he pulls back just enough to be able to kiss Lucas' lips. Then they press their foreheads together and sigh in unison. "Deal. I love you. I'm sorry. I'm so scared, Lucas. I'm all turned around."

Lucas hugs my brother again, rubbing his hand across the span of his back. "I know. But when we're scared, we run *to* each other, not *away* from each other. Got that?"

Declan nods, holding Lucas like a man who has just had his treasure returned to him. "I'm sorry."

"Forgiven and forgotten." Lucas turns his head to Rome. "Thank you."

Rome nods while his body oscillates to keep Miracle satisfied in his arms. "We're all we have. We can't go throwing that away."

Lucas leaves Declan to kiss Miracle's head, cupping the back of it like a man who desperately wants to be an uncle. "When you spit up, aim it at your Uncle Declan. That'll be my revenge for his freak out."

Declan chuckles as he resumes his spot before me and picks up the tweezers. He swipes at the condensation beneath his eyes. "Thank you," he whispers as Lucas leaves the room to go deal with Orlando.

"Tell Nico he's got the two of you to contend with for favorite uncle now." It's then I realize that in all the chaos, I haven't seen Nico since I got to the mansion. I would have thought he would be throwing a fit about my blood entering the house.

At the mention of Nico, Declan's expression closes off in time with Rome's.

"Where is Nico?"

Neither of them answers, which introduces me to a whole new set of worries.

If Nico is missing, it won't be long that he lasts in the hands of the angry members of the revolution.

9

MISSING NICO

Though I want to shout, I am too afraid of even my own volume. My voice is mousy now. "Where is Nico?"

Declan opens his mouth, but Rome's tone is sharp enough to shut it. "No."

Declan presses his lips together and continues plucking the glass from my skin, this time moving his attention back to my arms to do a final pass. "Drink that glass of water, Coco. You're dehydrated."

"I've had two already. Where is Nico?" Dread churns in my gut. I knew they were being too sweet. Too accommodating. "What happened?"

Rome shakes his head. "Nothing you can help with at the moment. We're dealing with it. Right now, this is where you need to be. It's where we all need to be. I've got people out searching for him."

I try to sit up straighter, but my stomach muscles aren't of much use. I'm lucky Declan propped me up on the bed with ample pillows, or I would have fallen sideways a while ago. "What? Did Nico get hurt in the fight? Did he get taken?"

Rome turns his chin from me, staring at Miracle instead. "His crew and every available person I can spare is out looking for Nico. He was taken by the revolution. They won't kill him; they would only risk taking him to draw you or me out. I anticipate getting the ransom call any minute now. Until then, we are doing all we possibly can to bring him home."

Panic leaps into my chest. As if Miracle can feel my fear, my poor baby starts to cry.

My uterus tugs in my gut, causing me equal amounts of emotion and physical turmoil. "I need Miracle! The baby is too far away."

Rome is cautious as he approaches, since I am still peppered with blood. "Careful."

My voice is laced with anxiety. "We have to find Nico. They're not going to go easy on him, Rome. Lampert's car crashed at the intersection of Maple and Klein, about an hour from here. He was heading east."

Rome nods. "I know. You said as much on the phone, and we sprang into action. My men are already scouring the area in that direction."

Declan stands from his chair, his lips drawing together as he thinks aloud. "They're heading east?"

Rome's head bobs. "They're at the intersection of the crash now, searching for clues as to where Lampert was headed."

My brain searches for details. "I heard Lampert telling Fintan he would be there with me in twenty minutes. If they took Nico to Fintan, then they've got to be holding Nico twenty minutes east of the crash."

Declan runs his hand over his face. "I know where Nico is at, then. Or at least, I have a pretty good guess."

Rome's head shoots toward Declan, his nostrils flared. "Where?"

"Steven Fairfax—Fintan's buddy—has an old warehouse he sometimes uses for poker nights. A bunch of guys used to meet up there semi-regularly when they wanted to hang out. You know, before you shot him. I don't know if that's the place the revolution might be stashing their prey, but the warehouse is in Dazier, which is east, about twenty minutes or so from Klein and Maple, if I'm remembering correctly."

Rome's arms stiffen. "Are you sure?"

Declan shakes his head. "Of course not. But if we're looking for places out of the way that fit that location's whereabouts you described, that's where I'd check first. I know Fintan has been there before."

Rome pulls out his phone with one hand and makes a call, barking out the narrowed location Declan gave him.

Declan is pale as he wipes my blood from the tweezers onto a towel. "I hate everything about this. I know I want us to find Fintan and free Nico, but I still hate it."

"That's because you're a good person. Don't let Fintan destroy that. We need you to care, otherwise, we're just a bunch of jaded survivors."

Declan kisses the top of my head, then dabs at the blood dotting my arms.

Rome pockets his phone, still swaying with Miracle in his arms. "It's okay. We'll find him. Lay back, little cannoli. You need to let your body relax. You've been through a lot."

We are one step closer to having our family all under one roof, but until Nico is home, I will not be able to rest.

10

AMAZING BODY

After Declan removes the last shard of glass from my arms and face, I am cleared to take a shower.

I'm not sure I can stand all that long, but my legs have been dripping with blood for the past hour, so I'll chance it.

Though, I have yet to put my feet on the floor, so it's more a theoretical effort at this point. My toes are dangling over the edge of the bed while Declan reminds me over and over to go slow, so I don't faint.

Rome is torn—I can see it on his face. He wants to help me in the shower, but he is also afraid to hand off Miracle to anyone.

I can't say I blame him. We have been through too much in Miracle's first few hours of life to risk being parted for even the briefest of moments.

"Declan, can you..." Rome makes to offer Miracle to

Declan to hold, but then pulls the baby back to his chest. "Never mind. I..." He shakes his head, turning to me with fear rounding his eyes. "I don't know how to do this. I don't know how to help you, which is something I always know how to do."

I shake my head. "I'm covered in blood, Rome. You shouldn't be helping me in the shower. I can do this."

Rome shakes his head. "No, you can't. But I can't put Miracle down, either. Like, I physically can't."

I press my feet to the floor, but use the edge of the bed as a crutch, feeling my way to the end of the mattress because I am worried I might fall. "I don't want you to. I'm bloody. You shouldn't be near me."

"Hold on, Sis," Declan insists.

Then my brother moves into the hallway and comes back seconds later with Lucas, who offers his hand to me with unending kindness radiating from him. "Declan said you might need help in the shower." Lucas glances at Rome, and then back at me. "Is that okay?"

I swallow hard and turn to Declan, silently asking him, as well, if that is okay.

It's weird, to be sure. But at this point, so many doctors have seen my vagina; I have very little sense of decency anymore.

Declan nods without a hint of hesitancy. "You need help in there. I'll change the sheets on the bed and make sure you can actually rest when you get out. I'll burn the linens, so there won't be an issue of your blood being out in the open. Your gown needs to be burned, too. Lucas can put it in a garbage bag for me."

Insecurity washes through me as I look up at Lucas, insecurity radiating out from me. "Are you sure?"

Lucas threads his fingers through mine. "One hundred percent. Let's get this mama into some clean clothes. Or into clothes that aren't a hospital gown."

Gratitude floods me as I take Lucas' hand and follow him down the hall and into the grand bathroom on the first floor of the Valentino mansion. The white marbled floors were pristine, but are now marred by the blood on my feet, which Lucas promises he will clean up.

He turns on the water, testing the temperature.

I try not to think about the fact that I am about to show my busted-up body to my brother's boyfriend. I try not to think of anything that might stay with me more than this moment.

Lucas keeps his judgment off his face, thank goodness. His hands are gentle, removing my gown and underthings slowly so I don't get spooked. My stomach is embarrassing, my legs are sporting several large puffs of purple from who knows which catastrophe. My arms look like they have been attacked by a cheese grater.

All these things are forcing me to be confronted with the trauma I have endured.

More tears drop down my nose as I watch Lucas strip down to his briefs. He moves into the shower and extends his hand, beckoning me to join him.

I hold my breath as I let Lucas guide me toward dignity.

For several whole minutes, we don't move or speak. We stand together while blood rinses down my legs and trickles down the drain.

When Lucas moves, it is only to kiss the back of my hand. It's his promise that he is not freaking out, so I don't need to, either.

It is a testament to how horribly depleted I am that I don't put up a fuss when Lucas gets down on his knees before me. Even as the blood pours from between my legs, he is careful with my body in ways that heal the fractured parts of my psyche.

"I'm sorry you have to do this!" I fret.

Lucas tilts his head, blinking up at me. "You're my family. I told Declan and now I'm telling you: I'm in this."

Just when I think I cannot be any more undeserving of such kindness, Lucas wins my heart when he starts to sing.

"*It's easy to get there,*
   It's easy to win.
   It's easy to wonder,
   But it's hard to begin."

I CUP MY HAND OVER MY MOUTH AS HIS WORDS WASH OVER me. Lucas' voice is low and beautiful, lulling my warring emotions into a docile state. I can still feel them, but they aren't in my face, screaming for me to understand or deal with them in a civilized manner before I am capable of such things.

My baby was born. That in and of itself is a miracle I cannot wrap my entire mind around.

The things the doctors shouted to each other during the birth echo in my mind. Maybe I suppressed them. Maybe I haven't had the time to ponder them. But now that I have this moment, this minute, I cling to the details that make this my story. I want to print it across my brain so I can tell Miracle the high and low points of their crowning moment. There is nothing I can do but be grateful we made it through the impossible.

And everything about this truly was impossible.

Miracle wasn't supposed to be able to be conceived, yet we did it. My body took a chance on Rome, betting on a path we didn't realize existed. My body fought to change history in ways no one could have predicted.

Not just because of who Rome is, but because of what my body has already been through do I feel grateful to be standing here in this shower.

When I look down now, I don't feel ashamed of my deflated, flappy stomach anymore. "My body is amazing," I whisper when Lucas finishes his song, humming lightly while the water falls.

Lucas looks up at my face with a smile. He stands and wraps his arms around me, pressing a kiss to my shoulder.

"Absolutely. Your body loves you. Your body is fighting for you."

My vision dims around the edges in time with my heart swooning at Lucas' words.

The warm water is nice and necessary, but I can feel my heart slowing.

I hold onto Lucas as I look up at him, reveling in the wonder of how lucky I am to be standing here. "I did it. I had a baby." My eyes close as my breath turns far more labored than simply standing should require. "I never thought I could do that."

Lucas keeps his arms around me. "I want all the details. After we get out of here, we'll sit and talk about it. Colette? Hun, are you alright?"

The heat from the shower was fine a second ago, but now it's overwhelming. Oxygen is hard to come by, and my knees weaken without my permission.

It's as if the moment I let myself feel safe, my body decided to check out.

After all, it's fought long enough.

All I hear are Lucas' shouts for Declan to come quick before the world floats away, dismissing me from my pain, if only for now.

MOTHER AND FATHER

Waking up naked in the shower with a flask shoved between my teeth isn't the best way to come to.

Orlando's jaw is firm as he leans over the edge of the tub, staring at my face with true worry rounding his features. "Her eyes are open," he calls over his shoulder.

I am sprawled out in Lucas' arms in the bathtub while the water pelts down on us. "Not good," I mumble as I take stock of my faculties.

"You fainted," Lucas informs me. "I'm guessing blood loss is the culprit? Or maybe the car crash. Or maybe giving birth and not having a proper break. Or maybe..." He presses his chin to the top of my head. "Or maybe it was a combination of the many obvious things."

I swallow down the last of Orlando's blood from the

flask, fully aware that I am still nude. "Well, this is embarrassing."

Orlando runs his rough knuckle across my cheek. "Let's get you dressed and into bed."

"Nico," I protest, my voice weak but my stubbornness in full swing.

Orlando's mouth tightens. "There is nothing you can do to help that situation. We're already handling it. Sleep. That's all you need to do right now."

I chew on my lower lip, looking for a loophole which might allow me to be helpful. I keep coming to a wall. Then again, my mind isn't exactly laced with focus.

Urgencies pop into my awareness at random. "Miracle? My baby is still safe?"

Orlando nods. "On my life, nothing will happen to your baby."

My big sweetie pie leans his forehead to mine over the ledge of the tub, connecting me to him in ways no one other than Rome has ever poked at his heart.

It's an effort in discomfort for all involved, I'm sure, but the three of us manage to get me dried, bandaged and dressed in fluffy, loose, long pajamas that bring a little civility to the situation.

Every part of me that has an open cut is covered with clothing, except the slices on my face, which Declan tends to with a healing sealant so dots of my blood don't get on any vampires.

Orlando guides me slowly down the hallway to a

different bedroom that doesn't have remnants of my blood in it. The room is simply decorated with gold leaf embellishments along the baseboards. The gold print is on the posts of the large bed and lining the dark wood nightstand.

Orlando is careful with me as he helps me get into the bed, even going so far as lifting my feet to rest on the mattress. Then he covers me with a blanket. "Rome is changing Miracle's diaper," Orlando explains. "They'll be right in." Then he lowers his head, his hands going behind his waist like a soldier awaiting a dressing down.

I'm not sure if he is waiting for me to start up a conversation or dismiss him so I can sleep. "Thanks, Orlando."

Still, Orlando doesn't move from the spot in the center of the room.

"Everything okay, Orlando my love?" I ask him. I know something is on his mind, other than the obvious horrors at hand.

Orlando replies without caveat. "I dropped you."

I scoff that this is the crux of his internal agony. "You were shot."

"You'd just given birth and I dropped you."

I stare him down. "Again, you were shot. How invincible do you imagine you are?" I motion for him to sit on the edge of the bed, which I am realizing has layers and layers of sheets to make for easy cleanup in case I bleed on them.

Even after Orlando sits beside me, he still won't look at my face, so I reach out and hold his hand.

"Does your leg hurt? Declan got the bullet out, right? But you were limping in the hallway."

"It's fine. It'll heal. Declan's getting good at fishing out bullets."

I snort at the compliment to my brother. "I'm sure it's a skill not many have had this much practice with in so short a time." I squeeze Orlando's hand, but my strength is paltry. Still, Orlando knows me, so he turns his head in my direction, his wounded puppy eyes letting me know that no matter if I don't hold him accountable or not, he will not forgive himself for dropping me.

"Orlando my love." My voice is soft. "Lie down."

"Huh?"

"You were just shot. Your cousin is missing. Lie down." When it becomes clear he won't rest to take care of himself, I switch tacks. "I need to rest, and I don't want anyone coming for me while I sleep. They won't come for me if you're here. Lie down. Rest with me."

Orlando glances at the door and nods. He's in his undershirt and black trousers when he turns off the light and climbs onto the side of the bed nearest the door. His gun rests on the nightstand, ready to defend us if need be.

I waste no time cuddling up to him, stretching my arm across his broad chest. No one would ever guess that Orlando is cuddly, but the feel of his steady breathing beside me finally lulls my eyelids to close.

Orlando kisses the top of my head while my cheek rests on his chest. "Sleep well, Colette my dove."

And finally, I do.

I am awoken I'm not sure how long later by the sound of my baby squawking. There's a heaviness to my chest, my breasts firm and painfully tender to any movement.

I roll away from Orlando, who is snoring, utterly spent.

I can't sit up on my own without it being a whole production, so I lay on my back and glance around the room, my eyes landing on Rome in a chair in the corner, shushing Miracle.

"Sorry," he says to me with an exasperated half-smile. "Go back to sleep."

"I can't. I think this is what it feels like when the baby needs to nurse." I make to rub my breasts because they are so sore, but that only makes them hurt more.

Rome's eyes widen. "Oh! That's good because Miracle won't take a bottle yet."

I scramble to sit up, losing my balance after two attempts. "They're starving!" I croak, finally managing to claw my way to sit up against the headboard.

Luckily, Orlando could sleep through a thunderstorm when he is thoroughly exhausted, so my movements don't disturb his slumber.

Rome comes to my other side and carefully hands the baby to me. He helps me get situated in silence.

There are a few touch and go moments, but eventually I learn how to nurse my baby.

My uterus contracts so painfully as Miracle sucks, that I reach out and grip Rome's shirt over his chest, my mouth open in a silent scream. I don't want to wake Orlando, so I bury my face in Rome's neck until Miracle gets a better latch.

The waves of discomfort keep me from relaxing, but that is nothing to the wonder that is holding my child. Finally, I have my Miracle in my arms.

"You're a natural at this mom thing," Rome informs me in a whisper once Miracle nurses less voraciously, enough that I can relax against the headboard. "I, on the other hand, was told I'm hovering too much." He gives a pfft noise that announces his disbelief.

I lean my head to Rome's shoulder, sighing contentedly that we made it through what I hope is the worst that life will dare to throw our way.

"We're parents," I announce in a whisper, marveling at the truth that sounds too grand to be real. "I'm a mother."

"You are." Rome's arm curves around my back. "And I'm a father. Funny how life twists."

"Funny indeed."

Rome's phone buzzes, taking him from my side so he can speak in short, clipped sentences near the door, so I don't eavesdrop on things that would only upset me.

"Obviously not. No. Out of the question." He glances at me, worry tightening his mouth. "I'll take care of it."

When he ends the call, I give him a purposefully naïve look. "Anything you care to share, honey? Was that someone calling to congratulate us?"

Rome rolls his tongue over his top row of teeth before

shoving aside his anger so he can give me a sweet reply. "That's exactly what it was, my little cannoli. Where should I have them send the flowers?"

"To wherever it is you have to rush off to, I assume with backup that hasn't recently been shot."

Rome runs his hand over his face, his whisper pained when it reaches me. "I can't leave, but I have to. If you thought I was overbearing when we were dating, and then insufferable when you were pregnant, me stepping out of this house when you and Miracle are sitting in bed so sweetly is impossible."

I press my lips together, knowing Rome well enough to understand that he needs me to order him away. Whatever this phone call is, he has to take care of it, or unthinkable consequences will occur.

"Go," I tell him in a quiet voice. "I've got Orlando here, plus a doctor. Where are Declan and Lucas?"

"Declan had to go to work, but he'll be back after. Lucas is cleaning up, but then he has to go to his job, too." Rome motions around the room. "This place locks down like a fortress. You remember the code for the alarm?"

"I've been living here for five months, and you ask me that every single time you're nervous." I chew on my lower lip. "Was that word on Nico?" My voice turns quiet. "What do they want?"

Rome leans against the wall, his eyes closing because life is not ready to grant him a sliver of reprieve. "The usual. You for him. If they don't see you at the drop off in half an hour, they'll send me a pint of Nico's blood. Then they'll start sending limbs."

Whatever calm my nap afforded me, I am miles from peace now. "We have to get him back, Rome."

He nods, his face tight with pain. "I will." Rome crosses the bedroom and kisses my forehead. He fishes in the drawer and tugs out a pad of paper, scribbling a note that he tucks into Orlando's pocket.

He kisses our Miracle on the top of their head while our baby drinks, their eyelashes fluttering contentedly.

"Stay here," he warns me. It's not a request but a firm command that, once I hear it, I am hesitant to obey.

I want to argue, but when he walks out the door, I still haven't found a reason to insist I go along.

But minutes after I know he is gone, unrest settles in my chest, so much that Miracle fusses, sensing my anxiety.

Whatever Rome is walking into, I worry he will not make it back alive.

12

NOT THE FUN UNCLE

Orlando stirs beside Miracle, who nursed themself to sleep forty minutes ago. He rubs his chest and then turns his head, startling when he sees the baby snuggled up between his body and mine.

"Don't let me do that!"

"What?" I look around to see what the cause of Orlando's unrest could possibly be.

"You let me sleep next to the baby! I could have rolled over and squished them!"

I relax back into the mattress. "I was awake. I would have stopped you."

Orlando sits up, facing away from us, his shoulders tight. "I'm no good with babies. I haven't been around any since Nico was one. I'm not the fun uncle."

I snort at his fretting. "No, you don't say." I shake my

head at him. "Orlando, honestly. You haven't even held the baby yet."

Orlando shoves his hands in his pockets. "And it's just as well. I dropped you, if you recall."

"You were shot!" I retort for what feels like the millionth time. "Look, I have to go to the bathroom. Can you please watch Miracle while I'm in there?"

Orlando looks afraid—truly frightened of the prospect of being near a baby. "I'm not the fun uncle," he repeats.

"I don't need you to be anyone but yourself. You're good at keeping me safe. Can you do that for all of five minutes for Miracle?"

Orlando gives me a look filled with hesitation, but finally nods. "They can just lie there, right? They're sleeping."

I nod. "Easy-peasy."

Orlando purses his lips but doesn't offer up a further protest. He pulls out his phone to check his messages while I make my way to the bathroom. I hope one of those texts are from Rome, assuring Orlando that all is well, and he is on his way home with Nico right now.

Of course, that is too much to ask of the universe.

By the time I emerge, Orlando is tugging on a shirt, his expression all business. "You'll stay here," he warns me, just like his cousin did. "Alarms set, you in this room. No matter what, this is where you stay."

I straighten as much as I am able. "Care to share what

you've heard? I know Rome must have touched base with you."

Orlando looks away as he tucks in his shirt.

Worry creases my brow. "He would have called me if he was on his way home, or if there was good news to report. He texted you, and he left a note in your pocket."

Orlando frowns, pulling out the letter that has tempted me for the last forty-five minutes. His eyes widen as he reads the hastily scrawled message, then crumples it in his fist, his bicep tight with anger.

"What?" I beg. "Orlando, what's happening?"

Orlando presses his fist with the balled-up note to his forehead, his eyes closed. "Rome, you idiot." He exhales through what I can tell is a list of things he needs to put in place to fix whatever has gone wrong.

"What happened? What did he do?" My stomach feels hollow and my body cold with fright.

When Orlando motions for me to come to him, I don't hesitate. I beeline for his arms, my face buried in his burly chest.

He grips the back of my head, his mouth moving atop my hair. "You'll stay here, understood? Right here. We take care of what's out there, and you take care of the miracle. Those are the zones."

I nod. "Where's my purse? I'll need a gun if I'm going to defend the house."

"It won't come to that," Orlando assures me, but my frown directed up at him makes it clear that I am not going to be okay with chancing it. "Your purse is in the living room."

I nod, leaning up on my toes to kiss his cheek. "Bring them home, Orlando my love."

He rubs his hand up and down my back, communicating more worry that I can only guess at. "Stay here, Colette my dove."

I agree because I have no other option. I agree because none of this makes a lick of sense. Paulo is at the hospital for his gunshot wound, along with Liesl.

I don't know who Rome took with him to bring Nico home, but there must be someone. There is no way Rome would have gone after Nico without solid backup.

After Orlando leaves, I call through the vast home, realizing that I am alone with my Miracle.

I move into the living room, grabbing my gun out of my purse, readying for whatever comes next.

13

FINTAN'S DEAL

I try not to think about my father, but when I am alone and the world is quiet, my mind wanders into dark corners where it shouldn't.

I don't know what sort of grandfather the sheriff would have been. Staring up at the oil painting of Daddy Valentino hanging in the living room, I know he would have been the sort to take Miracle out for ice cream and come back with a sack full of toys they don't need. That's how he was with me. I had only to glance at something that I fancied, and he would send it to the cashier for us to take home. He played dolls with me, not just bought them. I loved his proper attempt at a female voice, and the way he gushed over the pretend tea I served at our tea parties.

I cannot picture the sheriff doing anything like that with Miracle, mostly because he never did that sort of thing with me.

Miracle coos against my chest, where they have been for the past hour.

No update. No word from any of them. No nothing for an hour.

Neither Daddy Valentino nor the sheriff would sit back and tolerate that.

But I gave my word that I would stay put, so here I am, sitting with my baby in the mansion without a clue as to what chaos is raining down on the men I love outside these doors.

I take a sip from the flask of Orlando's blood and then place it back in the double-wide fridge. I hum to Miracle the song that Lucas sang me in the shower, but I think we both know the melody isn't covering my nerves.

When my phone rings, I practically jump on the thing. I have Miracle cradled in one arm as I press the device to my ear with the other. "Rome, thank God."

But it's not Rome's voice that answers. My spine straightens when Fintan's voice hits my ear. "I wouldn't go thanking God just yet, kiddo."

"Fintan?" I breathe, clutching my baby tighter.

My heart skips several very important beats as my eldest brother speaks in a controlled and firm voice over the phone. "How's my niece?"

"My baby is your nothing. Where is my husband?"

"Husband?" Fintan clucks his tongue. "You know vampires and humans can't marry. If you are referring to the abomination I used to call Rome, he is none of your concern anymore."

I remain silent, for fear of saying the wrong thing and making the situation worse for everyone I love who is trapped in Fintan's sphere.

My brother controls the conversation. "You know it doesn't have to go like this, right? I don't have to take the Valentino boys to get to you if you just come willingly."

Again, I say nothing, though I feel sick with rage and terror.

"I take it that's a no? I take it you want to listen while I torture your childhood playmate?"

I say nothing because if Fintan knows how acutely I feel this anguish, he will never tire of torturing Nico.

I grip the phone when I hear Nico wailing in the background. I don't know how to help him, other than give myself up. But I know that the first thing Fintan will do with my blood is murder Nico in front of me and make me watch while he dies.

No matter what I do, Nico is doomed.

I set Miracle down in the bassinet that I moved into the living room. I hate putting them down, but I fear Miracle will feel the rage vibrating through my bones.

Fintan takes a casual tone. "I hear congratulations are in order. Tell me what I need to know, Coco. Boy or girl? Are you the Last Deadblood, or do we have another blood donor?"

I say nothing, though I itch to curse him to the

condemned afterlife for which I know he is destined. Nothing I say or do will accomplish a single thing. Fintan will not stop until every vampire is dead.

"Why?" I finally whisper. "Why do you hate them?"

Fintan chuckles, as if I am naïve, and too small for the greater truths of the world. "They are a danger to us, Coco. I'm sure you of all people know that more than most. You've seen their fangs up close."

It's the same ignorant rhetoric that gets spewed in the media whenever there is a rare vampire attack. I don't know why I expected something more original, but there it is. "I didn't realize you'd gone predictable. I thought all this time there was a deeper reason for you being this way. Money and fearmongering? That's all you've got? You'll turn into a monster over average vices? That's who you are: average?"

Fintan's voice turns grim. I can tell he is walking away from other people so he can have a more private venue in which to take my good medicine and promptly spit it back out.

"You know I lost Liz to a rabid vampire. You know they're dangerous."

I scoff at his flimsy logic. "First off, you cheated on Liz more than you were actually with her. Don't get all precious about her memory when you were a crap boyfriend while she was alive. It was a tragedy what happened to her, but every vampire in the world does not deserve to have to pay for one rabid vampire's crime."

Fintan doesn't want to hear anything close to the truth. "Listen, Coco, you don't know what it's like to be the first-born. I have the family's legacy to protect. I had to deal with Dad's temper when he couldn't control the vampire problem anymore. You have it easy with your free designer clothes and your business that people flock to all so they can gawk at you. Some people actually have to work for a living."

"And this is work? Abducting people and trying to commit mass-murder? This is your grand plan for life?" My upper lip curls as I pace the living room. "And I don't know if you recall, but you have a brother, Fintan. Your brother works for a living without having to do anything illegal. Imagine that. These are your choices, not ones you had no autonomy over."

I shouldn't be talking. I should let my brother ramble to buy Orlando and Rome more time, if that is what they need so they can escape.

Fintan's voice turns sadistic. "Nico is good sport. He never tires, no matter what we do to him."

My stomach churns. "You're sick. Why are you so afraid of vampires when *you* are the one hurting people?"

Fintan growls into the phone. "They're not people! Don't you get that? The baby you gave birth to isn't a person; it's an abomination."

My blood runs cold as some baser emotion rises up in me. I have felt the need to defend my territory and my loved ones before, but this is different. There is a savage note to my temper now.

I rock Miracle's cradle with my foot when they start fussing, though the motion is more to calm myself than my baby.

"Quite the uncle you are, talking like that. My baby is only a tool to you, then? You're so bigoted and small-minded that you can't see your niece or nephew for the family they are?"

"Stop dancing around it, Coco. What is it? Boy or girl?"

"My baby is none of your concern," I spout, parroting back his earlier words. "Send Nico home and we can talk, but you will never meet my baby after calling them an abomination."

Fintan clucks his tongue at my obstinance. "Shame you won't cooperate. Tell me, how long do you think it will take a vampire to heal from a bullet to the brain? Shorter than it took for you to heal from your head injury, sure, but do you think Rome will be aware of what's going on when I kill his brother in front of him?"

I go silent once more, closing my eyes because I cannot believe this is my brother. This is the family nature saw fit to give me.

I guess they can't all be Declan.

"I'm betting it's an hour before Rome is coherent. It's a good thing for you that we're out of your blood, but maybe a bad thing for the Valentino brothers. Now we get to play for hours. Days. Maybe even years. As soon as they get up, they get another bullet. You would think I would get tired of it, but it's fantastic entertainment."

My entire body quakes with rage as tears wet my eyes. "You're a monster!" I whisper through gritted teeth.

"No, Coco. They are the monsters. They are animals, and nothing more."

"Rome was your best friend! What did he ever do to you? My baby deserves their father!"

Fintan's voice loses all traces of merriment. "He left me behind. When Rome came into his family's fortune, I went to him for help. I needed money to get my loan business off the ground. Just seed money I would give him back once the business started turning a profit. You wouldn't guess that your boyfriend is a tightfisted bastard, would you."

I can't believe my brother is talking like this. Or maybe I can believe it, but I don't want to. I don't want to think anyone, save for some man with a curled mustache and a villainous laugh, could behave so appallingly.

I close my eyes, grasping at any tool at my disposal that might bring the Valentinos home. "Fintan, please. I need you to stop this." I clench my fist at my side. "I'll give you money. You can have the trust Mom left to me. Give me back Rome and Nico. Please, Fintan. The money is yours."

Fintan pauses, clearly not having considered that I might be good for something other than my blood. "I wouldn't mind that. How much is in there?"

"A million," I promise without a blink.

"Huh," he remarks, as if not expecting me to have saved anything from our mother for this long. "I think I might be able to trade Nico for a million, though he's not worth a tenth of it."

"For both of them, Fintan. You know I want them both home safe."

"No dice. Rome is the one you think you love. He's worth ten times what you'll pay for Nico."

I pinch the bridge of my nose as I pace the living room. "You know I don't have that!"

Fintan chortles at my frustration. "You will find it if you want to see Rome again. I'll part with Nico for a million, but it'll be ten for Rome. Wire transfer. Every hour I don't see the money in my account, one of them gets a bullet. It's on you how much blood they lose." His tone feigns innocence just to mock me. "I hear it's bad for a vampire to lose blood. I hear that's how they turn rabid." He tsks me. "I would hurry if I were you. Wouldn't want them to cause any deaths that the press would most certainly cover. Might set your ridiculous peace movement back a few decades."

I speak through gritted teeth. "Give me time to get the money, dumbass."

"I don't care how long it takes you, Coco. I'm in no rush. I could watch the Valentino brothers scream on their knees for days. Call me when you have the money ready to transfer."

I am sweating when the phone call ends. I circle the

living room, pacing nervously while I call my bank and make the necessary arrangements. A million is nothing for Nico's life, but I have no idea where I could possibly get ten million dollars.

Bile rises in my esophagus when I call Orlando. "Fintan has them both," I announce with no finesse. "He wants a million for Nico and ten million for Rome. He's going to shoot one of them every hour until he has his money."

Orlando cusses. "Your brother is sick."

"Granted. I have the million that I can transfer for Nico, but I'm guessing you'd be upset if I handled the pickup."

"You'd be right. You're still in the mansion, doors locked?"

"Yes." I chew on my lower lip and pick up Miracle from their cradle. My movements are careful as I take them into the nearest bedroom.

Premature. That's what the doctors said. Miracle should be tended to in a hospital, in case something isn't quite developed yet. The doctor praised Miracle's organs, and other than jaundice, said they were a perfectly healthy, albeit small, baby. Blame it on resilient vampire genetics or blame it on fate cutting us a break.

Still, I know my baby should be around nurses, not dealing with abductions.

I can hear Orlando's car's engine. I know he is trying to find his way to his cousins.

"Orlando, I don't know how to get my hands on ten million dollars."

"It's in your account. Or, it will be in the next five minutes. Tell Fintan the drop-off needs to happen now. You make the transfer when I tell you. Tell him you've got the money and you're ready to make the trade. Once I see Rome and Nico alive and in person, I'll call you in front of Fintan to have you complete the wire transfer."

"That's how this sort of thing is done? What if I make the transfer and they don't give them up?"

"Then we're out eleven million dollars. I don't care about the money. We need to get them back."

"Agreed. This will do that? You're sure?"

"I'm not sure about anything, except that Rome is a father. He needs to come home."

I nod, holding back any obvious emotion in my tone. "Fintan told me he's out of my blood. He needs more. So if he shoots, more likely than not, it's not lethal."

"That's good to know. You're safe? You're staying put?"

"You told me to stay here and watch over Miracle, so that's where I am. Fintan won't get his hands on my baby."

"Good. Never forget that's what he wants. He wants your blood. I'm surprised he's willing to give up the guys so easily."

"You call eleven million dollars easy?"

"I call it shortsighted, if Fintan's true goal is to eradicate us."

"But Fintan doesn't want Rome or Nico. Not really. He

wants my blood." I grimace. "My brother wants my blood because he needs to sell it for money. He's in a lot of debt."

"Right. So this trade is going to get him what he needs."

I lower my chin. "He called my baby an abomination."

Orlando's growl is low in his throat, but no less predatory. "I'll make sure he eats those words before I kill him." He pauses and then delivers the hard truth. "That's my way of telling you that your brother is not going to live through this exchange. I'm sorry, Coco. No one snatches at a Valentino and lives to brag about it. He has to be put down."

I chew on my lip. "I know. Do what you have to. Bring the guys home, Orlando my love."

"Hold tight, Colette my dove."

Though no part of me wants to go through with this trade, I call Fintan, hoping I have enough collateral for him to send the Valentino men home alive.

14

MIRACLE'S FATHER

Half hour passes after I put in the call to Fintan, and there is still no word from anyone on the status of the exchange. My phone is charged and my nerves have hit their peak, but still, I have received no word from Orlando that the trade is happening.

Declan promised to come over after work, and Lucas said the same, but they still have an hour more before I can expect them to be here.

On top of that, I have an infant who needs me.

I don't know how to take care of a baby. I've never even babysat before. I read loads of books during my pregnancy, but I recall none of their wisdom now.

Miracle wants to be held. If they are in my arms, they are fine. But it seems that now if I put Miracle down for the briefest of seconds, they start fussing and then screaming.

I can't say I blame them. Their first two days of life

have been nonstop panic. This is the time I am supposed to be Mother Earth on a lily pad, basking in the glow of just having birthed the most perfect baby in the universe.

Instead, I am huddled in the corner of a guest bedroom, frightened my brother is going to murder the father and the uncle of my baby.

"You will not grow up without your daddy," I promise Miracle as I hold them in my arms. I cannot imagine my thumping heart's erratic beating is soothing to my baby, but whenever I put them down, they don't like it.

I can already tell I'm going to be a sucker for this child.

Fine by me.

I sing Lucas' lullaby to Miracle, my voice pinched as a lump rises in my throat. I am terrified I won't get any call at all, or that I will get the last call I could ever want to hear.

I am used to being the one who is abducted, not the one praying for news that my family has been found alive.

"I remember the first time I kissed your father," I tell Miracle, finally finding my voice. Singing to them is no big deal, though my singing voice is nothing to brag about. But talking to my baby? I haven't done a whole lot of that yet.

Then again, we've had an audience from the beginning. This is our first time truly alone.

"We're not alone," I assure my Miracle. "Daddy's coming home soon. I don't want you to worry, though. He might have some ketchup spilled on his clothes and he might be limping. That's okay. Daddy will always be here for us." My eyes wet because apparently now that I have given birth, I will never be able to turn off my emotions.

Miracle looks up at me with lidded eyes, their round cheeks pink and perfect, as if asking for more of my voice.

So I talk to my sweet baby, imparting not a trace of my wisdom, but instead doling out a pure dose of my recklessness.

"Being with anyone wasn't in my plan. It couldn't be. I wasn't supposed to live this long. Every year I was granted was a gift I knew I couldn't waste. But when your father came along, everything I thought I could control finally slipped out of my grip." I hold my sweetheart to my chest as tears fall freely. "When your father walks into a room, I know it. When he stares at me, I feel it. We should never have connected, but we did, and now there will never be any undoing it." I kiss Miracle's forehead. "He will be back soon. Don't you worry. He loves us too much for anything to stop him. Not bullets, not politics, not the world."

Miracle makes a precious cooing noise as if they understand how rare it is to find a love like ours, for us to have found each other and then created our very own dream out of pure love.

"He will come for us," I assure my baby as much as I promise myself. I am not sure which of us needs to hear those words more, so I say them again. "He will come for us."

I kiss my baby yet again, loving the softness of their face.

Five pounds, three ounces. My baby weighed five pounds, three ounces at birth. Even though the doctor said their respiratory system was fully developed, thanks to their vampire DNA filling in the gaps where a human baby might experience a few setbacks, I still watch my baby like a hawk for signs that anything might be a struggle for them.

"My life was different before I met your daddy. I mean, there was plenty of this nonsense," I tell Miracle, motioning around to indicate the life that has gone wrong on so many accounts. "But before him, I was all business. All work and no play. I'm sure nobody would guess that Rome Valentino has a playful side to him, but he does, and he dusts it off to display it for me." I nuzzle Miracle's nose. "And now for you. If you would have told me two years ago that Rome Valentino would have fallen in love with a human, settled down and had himself a baby, I would have told you that you were crazy. Yet here we are—two of the few sane people in this mess."

Miracle makes a cooing noise that causes my heart to swell. That precious sound pushes out the creeping images that keep coming into my mind of Rome and Nico all bloodied and beaten.

When my phone rings, I nearly shout into it, startling my baby. "Yes? Where do I send the money?"

My mother's money. The money she set aside for me from her hard work spent trying to bring peace between the vampires and the humans.

At least she can rest in peace, knowing the money she left me is going to free a vampire. And one from the family she loved, no less.

Her heart would never stop breaking if she knew that Fintan was the culprit, pulling the strings of the public to paint vampires in a damning light.

If only Fintan cared that it is our mother's money he is extorting from me.

He truly is lost, and has been for longer than I realized.

At least the sheriff isn't alive to see this.

Orlando reads me the number of the account to which I am to send the money. Eleven million dollars, gone in a matter of a minute.

And worth every penny if it means getting my boyfriend and his brother back alive.

"It's done," I tell him, grateful I can maneuver my phone with one hand, so I don't have to put down my Miracle. "Tell Fintan to check his account."

Orlando holds the phone away from his head and shouts across what I assume is a divide—our people on one side and Fintan's on the other. I can picture a creepy warehouse in the late-night light, where Fintan arranged for the exchange to take place.

Fintan should be on my side, by my side. He should love me better than this, or at all. But I guess when one's soul corrodes, it has precious little softness left for those who should matter.

I have Declan as my family. He's the best one, anyway.

Declan is all I need from my side of the family tree. He's all anyone needs.

"No!" Orlando shouts, scaring me because it is clear something has gone amiss in the plan.

I hold the phone away from my baby when gunshots rain down on the criminals and vigilantes alike, shedding more blood that I hope my baby never has to know about.

I clutch my baby to my chest, scared that the violence will never end. Miracle cries, jerking my heart around in my chest.

This will not be our family's legacy. There will not be a trail of blood behind the crib.

"Coco, help me," comes Orlando's gasp when the gunfire comes to a stop. "The revolutionaries are gone, but I've been shot. I can't drive, and the guys can't, either."

"They're alive? Rome is alive?"

"Yes. Hurry."

"On my way." I stand, my legs rubbery as I grab up my purse and toe on slippers. Miracle is coming with me, though I am certain this goes against every parenting book ever written.

My baby and I will bring home the men we love, and Fintan will pay for his crimes.

15

SMALL BABY, BIG MEN

Miracle and I make our way to the garage, where I try to get my tiny baby into the car seat for the first time by myself. My buttery fingers can't seem to stop trembling, though I know it's not my condition acting up. No, this is pure nerves. The car seat is enormous in comparison to my tiny baby.

Too small. The baby is too small to be going through any of this.

Miracle cries the second I situate them in the seat. They don't like not being I my arms, now that we've been reunited.

Nevertheless, I have to hurry. I buckle my baby and move quickly to the driver's seat. I'm in my pajamas when I pull out of the Valentino mansion, a wild look about me that hopefully warns all police officers not to pull me over when I am so near the edge of deranged.

My body is not even close to healed from the act of giving birth and then being abducted, then promptly heading into a car crash. Even driving a car pains my bones.

The drive takes forever. Each minute feels like the longest of my life. Miracle doesn't like to be put down, so they cry this horrid little squeak that apparently goes straight to my breasts. I gasp when my nipples begin to leak milk, but even that cannot distract me from getting where we need to go as fast as possible.

When I finally pull into the barely lit parking lot of an old warehouse, I see Orlando's sedan and two other cars. I throw the car into Park beside Orlando's, my lower lip quivering at the horrors I might find in the darkness.

I don't bother counting the bodies. I don't look for my brother to confirm he is dead.

There are only three men I want to see right now.

"Nico," I breathe, rushing to him despite my body telling me that is not something I should be doing. He is supine on the ground in a pool of his own blood. His shoulder is riddled with bullet holes. His shirt is gone, so I can see the wounds perfectly.

His eyes are closed, which is probably best. Being passed out from the pain is a blessing when the agony is this acute.

Orlando whistles to me from across the way. "I've got Rome."

"He's alive?" I cry as tears wet my eyes.

"He's alive, Coco. But we're all in bad shape. Can you get Nico into the car? They brought him out unconscious, so you should be safe."

I nod, though I am not sure I can pick up a full-grown man and move him several feet. Then I have to figure out how to lift him into the car.

One nightmare at a time.

Since I can't actually carry him, I take hold of Nico's ankles and drag him across the parking lot, grunting at the effort that I really don't have the stamina to sustain. My uterus is in agony, and my back rings of stiffness, but still I persist.

By the time I get Nico to the backdoor of the car, Miracle is shrieking for me, wondering why I am struggling to lift a grown man off the concrete when I could be snuggling them.

If only.

I grit my teeth and grunt, finally summoning the strength to slide Nico into the back beside Miracle.

Hopefully his presence will calm my baby down while I help Orlando with Rome.

My body is telling me to stop—warning me, is more like it. I know this does not constitute the bedrest my doctor prescribed, but that fact only serves to make me double down on my efforts to get Rome into the car.

I can rest when we get home. Declan will fish out the bullets and help the Valentino men get back on their feet.

I race to Orlando's side. "Tell me he's okay."

"He will be, but I need help. They got my bad leg and my shoulder, so I'm useless for lifting him. Can you bring the car around, so we don't have to drag him as far?"

"On it." I move as quick as I can back to the car. My breastmilk leaks through my shirt, adding a chill to my skin. My stomach aches so badly that I nearly cry out with every step.

When I open the door, I expect to hear Miracle's screams at being kept in the baby carrier. But there is a weakened squawk that tells me hopefully they are on their way to sleepy town.

But when I glance into the backseat after I shove the keys into the ignition, a scream the likes of which I didn't know I was still capable splits the night air. "Nico, no!"

Deranged from blood loss, Nico's mouth is suctioned around my baby's arm, his fangs piercing the skin while he drinks.

MY CHILDHOOD BEST FRIEND

I tear open the backdoor of the sedan as tears cloud my vision. No matter, I don't need to see Nico to tear his head off. "Nico, stop!" I scream at my childhood bestie, using my surge of adrenaline to jerk Nico by the arm so hard that he flops out of the backseat and onto the parking lot's pavement, slack jawed and limp.

Nico lays on the concrete while I climb over his body to get to my baby. I can't stop crying as I fiddle with the car seat's buckle. I scream for Orlando, for Rome, for Declan, for a doctor, for my mother herself to come down and save my baby.

"No! No, no, no. Miracle, I'm here! I'm so sorry. Please don't leave me! Open your eyes! It was an accident! I didn't think Nico would wake! Miracle, please!"

My baby's eyes close and my heart implodes, agony ripping me in two.

Orlando limps laboriously to the car, taking in the scene uncertainly. "What happened? What can I do?"

My mind races. "I don't know! Nico drank from Miracle."

"Is he dead?"

"I don't know! Miracle's not waking up, Orlando! Open your eyes, baby doll! I can't... Please!"

"My blood," Orlando reasons. He takes a swab with his finger from the bullet wound on his leg and presses it between Miracle's tiny lips. He rubs the blood on their tongue, but Miracle isn't swallowing.

I pop up the hem of my shirt and shove my breast into my baby's mouth, hoping that will coax them to swallow what I hope is lifesaving medicine.

Orlando's breath is heavy across my neck, which I know means he is fighting with consciousness.

I hold the air in my lungs, refusing to breathe if my baby does not draw breath with me.

The pain of nursing is the best relief I could possibly feel. I grip Orlando's shirt by the buttons, bracing myself because Miracle's jaw is strong. "Nursing," I tell him, breathless as tears stream down my face. "Alive."

Orlando exhales, burying his face in my hair. "That's one of us on the road to healing. Good." He drops to his knees, but it's not because he has fainted. He kneels beside Nico, who I now notice is twitching on the concrete.

I cannot feel terror that this is Nico's last moment. I can't feel anything. I sob into the air, my chin lowered because my baby is alive, but I don't know how permanent that relief will be. I massage Miracle's chest, hoping to coax along their heart to replenish any blood that Nico took.

"Nico was rabid," I explain to Orlando. "He was passed out when I put him in the car. But he must have woken up when my back was turned. He drank from Miracle, Orlando!"

"It's a waiting game, then," Orlando says, his voice grim. "Either Miracle's blood is lethal, like yours, or you are the Last Deadblood."

I wail into the night air. "I didn't want to find out like this!"

"None of us did." Orlando reaches out and scoops up Nico's hand while my childhood bestie twitches in the night. His eyes roll back while his body jerks unnaturally.

I can't feel this. I can't feel all of it at once. The relief is marred with the fear of my baby not being out of the woods yet. Then there is the terror that Nico might die at the hands of my baby. Nico could breathe his last mere inches away from me.

I don't want to watch my childhood best friend fade away at the hands of my baby.

I pray with everything in me that I am the Last Deadblood. I don't want this life for Miracle. The world isn't good enough to be trusted with another generation of a weapon this deadly.

Orlando lets out a bleat of worry that turns my already contracting stomach. I try to keep my arms steady for

Miracle to maintain the business of nursing, turning my head only slightly so I can witness what I hope is not Nico's last moment.

"Is he..." But I cannot finish that sentence.

Then Nico shocks us both when he shouts as if someone has punched him square in the stomach. Though he was beyond speech mere seconds ago, his energy, it seems, has renewed in full force.

Though if this is a triumphant recovery or Nico's last breath, I cannot tell.

ESCAPING

I don't understand what I am witnessing. Nico was convulsing on the pavement of the parking lot outside the starlit warehouse because he was rabid and drank some of my baby's blood. Then he cried out with what looked like renewed energy.

Now Nico's eyes are open as he stares up in wonder.

He's not dead. In fact, he looks shockingly coherent.

"Nico?" I whisper in the darkness, unsure if hope is a fool's journey.

"I..." Nico's voice is raspy but it's there. "I..." He lifts his hand without true muscle control, and Orlando grabs it.

Orlando helps Nico to sit up, but now it looks like Orlando is the one who needs assistance more than the younger man whose shoulder is peppered with bullets. Moments ago, Nico was rabid from thirst.

"You were convulsing," I tell Nico, astonished that he can comprehend speech.

Orlando limps to the trunk and pulls out a blood tab, sticking it to Nico's tongue and closing his mouth for him, as if Nico is a small boy.

Orlando is dripping with blood from his calf, but his focus is wholly on Nico.

"I don't understand," Orlando admits. "You're alive?"

It is said as a question, not because Nico doesn't look it, but because there is no possible way he could be this coherent this quickly, even if Miracle's blood isn't deadly. It's not like Miracle gave Nico enough blood to replenish all that was depleted. Yet Nico appears lucid, and can now sit up on his own while he sucks on the blood tablet.

Nico looks around from his spot sitting on the concrete of the warehouse's parking lot, as if seeing the world with new eyes. "What did you give me?"

Orlando smashes his lips together.

"You're controlled," I marvel. "You were just... and now you're..."

"I'm okay. Sore, but fine." He makes to move his shoulder and then winces. "On second thought, where's Declan? I need him to fish out some bullets." He breathes in deep through his nose. "Whatever you gave me is amazing. I barely feel anything. These gunshot wounds are like a bruise or something. I know the bullets are in there, but it's not all that painful."

Orlando struggles to keep himself upright against the side of the car. He skips over getting to the bottom of things in favor of getting out of here. "If that's the case, can you drag Rome over?"

"I reckon I can. Did you put a bullet in Fintan's brain?"

"No. I tried, but he got away."

My eyes close because I don't want to feel upset that my brother is still alive. I don't want my brother to be the kind of person the world would be better without.

Nico frowns. "Rat bastard. Don't worry, Orlando. We'll track him down."

It's odd, how normal Nico sounds. I know vampires don't always remember the things they've done in their rabid state, but his recovery from starved to coherent should take a whole lot more than a little of Miracle's blood (my baby doesn't have a ton to begin with) and a blood tab. What I am seeing is not possible.

Yet there Nico stands.

"You're okay," I state in disbelief, holding my baby in the backseat of the car.

Nico tilts his head to the side. "Of course I am, Sis. Nothing to worry about. Vampires don't get taken down by bullets like you would." He reaches into the car and swipes at my slick cheeks. "You were really that worried for me? You little softy. I'm okay."

"Home," I beg, my lower lip quivering. "I need to go home."

Nico nods, taking the wish as a directive. "Not a problem. I can drive one-handed. You look white a sheet. I don't trust you behind the wheel just yet. I'll call Declan on the way, so he can fish out these dang bullets. Annoying." He glances over his shoulder. "Let me get Rome."

Annoying? That's what Nico is feeling right now? I am torn between incredulous relief and railing at him because my baby almost died a mere minute ago.

Nico doesn't give me the chance to choose between those two options, though, because he is already moving to Rome's limp body across the way.

Orlando hefts himself into the backseat beside me, his larger body squishing me between himself and the baby seat. "What just happened? You saw that too, right?"

I nod, resituating Miracle to the other breast so their head doesn't bump against the car seat. I'm not exactly deft at this nursing thing, but Orlando is just distracted enough not to be weirded out when I try and fail over and over to shove my nipple into Miracle's mouth.

Finally, my baby latches, and I exhale.

"Alive," I rule. "They're both alive. I can't care about anything beyond that right now. I don't know how it happened, only that it did. I'm grateful the worst might be behind us."

"Yes, you do know exactly how it happened," Orlando replies gravely. "You told me yourself. Nico was rabid and drinking from Miracle's arm. There are his fang marks right there." He reaches down and tugs up my baby's arm, thumbing the injury that is too gruesome for me to stare at directly.

A sob I cannot control belts out of me, startling Miracle so much that they cry along with me. "I'm sorry!" I fret, trying to get Miracle to nurse again. I don't have words until I feel them latch once more. "I can't see my baby's arm torn up like that! I'm fragile, dammit!"

Orlando shushes me lovingly, even though he is in intense physical pain at the moment. His uninjured arm winds around my back so he can cradle my head against his chest. "Miracle is alive. Nico is alive. It's all okay."

I cry quieter this time, letting Orlando hold me because I cannot keep my composure through this life any longer. "I'm scared," I admit. "I'm so scared."

Orlando kisses the top of my head. "I know. We'll get Miracle home, and the doctor will fix them up."

I cry in small fits and starts as Nico hefts Rome into the car. My tears flow more freely once I see the state of Rome's face, which has been beaten with what looks like a bat or something equally solid. His nose is broken, his jaw off-kilter, and he is also sporting a bullet wound, but his is on his side.

Orlando covers my eyes with his palm, keeping my head lain against his chest. "Home," Orlando orders. "Nico, if you can't drive, let me know."

Nico snorts, though where he got his humor from, I'll never understand. I cannot imagine anything being funny ever again. "I've got it, Orlando. I could tap dance around you, old man. Keep the baby safe back there. That's your only job."

While I know Nico is saying it as a joke, guilt drapes itself around my shoulder.

My only job is to keep my baby safe. Miracle is in their second day of life, and I have already failed.

CRAZY TOWN

I cry the entire way home, so much that Declan has to take Miracle from my arms upon our arrival to the Valentino mansion, so I don't drop them.

Lucas helps the guys into the house one at a time, laying them down on the floor in the living room, where Declan has the most space to work.

I am manic, I realize, as I take Miracle back from Declan and hold them to my chest in the bedroom away from the others. I wince when the sounds of Rome wailing as Declan resets his broken jaw and nose fill the mansion.

I have locked everyone out, afraid of that horrible howling—afraid of everything I don't understand.

Nico drank Miracle's blood. I saw it. If Miracle is the Last Deadblood, Nico would be dead. But when we got into the house, Nico insisted Declan see the others first because he felt fine.

I guess I am still the Last Deadblood.

I exhale with relief. Once word gets out that Miracle cannot murder innocent vampires, my baby will not be a target of the revolutionaries.

I don't know how Nico is alive. Even without ingesting potentially lethal blood, he should be depleted of energy and barely moving, if the bullet holes in his shoulder are any indication of the trauma his body has gone through.

But Nico is whistling. I can hear the sound making its way down the hall.

I stare at my baby as I sit on the floor in the far corner of the guest bedroom, wondering at the logic in any of it.

Declan bandaged up my baby's arm upon our arrival home. He disinfected the puncture marks while peppering me with questions to which I still don't have answers.

I moved the nightstand in front of the bedroom door to barricade myself inside when I first entered the room. When I have the energy, I will move the bed (or I will try to, at least). I can't have another rabid vampire near my baby. Though, to be fair, Rome wasn't rabid when he came to on the way home, and Nico was cracking stupid jokes by the time he pulled into the driveway.

Still, I press my body into the far corner of the room, sitting on the floor, clutching my baby to my chest. I am done being reasonable. My butt is sore on the bare floor, but I don't care. I don't want comfort. I can't chance falling asleep, though my grip on consciousness isn't all that firm.

Miracle is content to coo in my arms, staring up at me and no doubt thinking, "Why is my mom so crazy?"

"I'll tell you why," I answer, knowing I have crossed the boundaries of sanity long ago. "Mommy is scared, that's why. If the world hurts you, then the world goes away. All of it. Everyone. They can find a different baby to fight over. We are staying in here, where no one can hurt you ever again."

My body aches all over. I am tired and wired, which is a bad combination. I want to check on Rome, but I can't chance being around people. Miracle needs to be protected from everyone and everything.

When a knock sounds on the door nearly an hour later, I growl at the intruder.

"Can I come in, tré-sur?"

"No!" I snap, though I don't mean to. "I'm lying down."

I don't have a plan. I just know that nothing is safe, and the outside world cannot be trusted with my perfect baby.

Rome's voice comes back to me with a hint of confusion. "Talk to me, little cannoli. Orlando explained what happened. Do you want me to ask Nico to step out for a bit?"

Yes.

No.

I don't know.

Nothing feels like an actual fix.

"I don't want anyone in here. Stay out until I have a

plan." I know I sound childish at best and crazy at worst, but that is the maniac I have become, I guess.

Rome's pause gives me the false hope that I might not have to give a further answer for my unbalanced behavior. But when his voice comes to me, low and commanding, I know I won't be able to stay in here much longer. "Coletta, I'm coming in." When he tries the door and finds the knob won't give, his frustration deepens his tone. "You locked me out?"

"You might have been rabid!" I protest.

"Well, I'm not. I'm not dangerous to you or to our baby, Coletta. You know this. Unlock the door, or I'll unlock it myself."

"You can't do that!"

"It's my house, tré-sur." Then he catches himself. "*Our* house. I have the keys to all the doors." To prove his point, he shoves the key into the lock and turns it. When the door hits the nightstand, he lets out a grunt of frustration. "Coletta, did you barricade yourself inside?"

"I told you I'm not ready for anyone to come in!"

"Lucas, give me a hand, here."

"Don't you dare!" My chin wobbles with the fear that Rome will see me like this—unhinged and without the answers I need to make it through this horrible time.

Lucas and Rome push their way inside. I can tell Rome is gearing up to yell at me, but the moment his eyes land on Miracle and me on the floor, huddled in the corner, he holds up his hands. "I won't come near, okay?"

I size up his steps and measure the space between us with my wide eyes. "Stay there."

Rome nods, then tucks one hand behind his back like a soldier. "Yes, Ma'am. I want to see you both. I have to make sure you're okay."

I scoff. "Do I not look okay?"

Rome's shoulders lower. "You look terrified."

Self-loathing claws at me. "Well, you're the one who should be scared! I almost let our baby die! I put a rabid vampire in the backseat with our baby! *I* am the danger, not Fintan. I am the one who will end the Deadblood legacy, not anyone out there who wants to snatch at my baby."

Rome looks on me with pure pity when he should be raging at my carelessness. He barely survived my brother and still bears the marks of the many beatings. He should be livid with me. "Coletta, I..."

"No! I don't want to hear your reasons why it's all fine." My chin wobbles. "I'm a terrible mother! I don't know how to do this! I left Miracle with Nico, and... and... That's basic vampire stuff any dummy knows not to do!"

Rome inches toward me, moving slowly while my lower lip quivers. "No one is mad at you," Rome promises. "We're just glad you're okay."

"Do I look okay?" I nearly yell at him, though I don't mean to.

Lucas gapes at me, clearly never having seen this side of me before.

To be fair, the unhinged side is new to me, too.

Lucas holds up his hands. "I'm not here to do anything but ask if you need Orlando's flask of blood. He is worried about you."

I am shivering, but I manage a nod. "I don't remember what day it is. I don't know when I drank last. Better safe than sorry."

Lucas taps his temple. "That's some solid logic."

Rome stands in place while Lucas crosses the room carefully. He gives me plenty of time to adjust to the idea that someone is encroaching on our space.

"You're trembling," Lucas points out. "Declan said you're not supposed to get like this."

I shoot him a scowl. "A lot of things weren't supposed to happen today."

"Fair point. I'm going to hold this to your lips, okay? Then you don't have to let go of Miracle."

Rome looks as though he might yell his anguish into the room. "If your arms are shaking, you shouldn't be holding the baby. Please, Coletta. Let Lucas hold Miracle, at least until you're steady enough for it."

"I'm not trembling; I'm cold. There's a difference." Though, to be honest, I can't tell anymore.

"Your adrenaline is crashing and you might be low on blood. Couple that with the fact that this isn't exactly bedrest, and you've got a recipe for, well, this." Rome motions to my crazed expression. "You can trust me. There is no one more important to me than the two of you. If I was going to attack a human, I would snack on Lucas here. He's closer."

Lucas shoots Rome a wry look over his shoulder. "Hey."

I clutch Miracle tighter to me, though I have no evidence to trust myself with my baby more than Rome. In fact, I am the one who made the near-fatal mistake of putting Nico near my baby and then turning my back on the two. I can't let go of Miracle. I am not capable of the feat.

"I can't," I admit. "I almost lost my baby tonight."

Rome sits down, though I can tell this costs him great pain as he grimaces and grunts like an old man.

"What did they do to you?" I ask with trepidation tightening my tone.

Lucas sits beside me and tips the flask to my lips, reminding me to swallow the crimson liquid my body needs.

My frame sags against Lucas as warmth coats my insides, relaxing my limbs in time with my exhale.

Lucas takes Miracle, but he doesn't move from my side, so my need to panic isn't as acute. "That's good. Just breathe."

"Where I can see them," I remind Lucas, who remains by my side with my Miracle in his arms.

Rome moves to my other side despite my trepidation so he can wrap his arms around me.

Everything I have been holding tight to collapses in a

gust of grief and relief as I sag in Rome's arms. Even though he has been through horrors I can only imagine, he holds me as if there is nothing more to life than the two of us.

The three of us.

"I'm scared," I whisper.

"I'm here," Rome promises. "Whatever comes, we will handle it together. Not with you barricading yourself in a room. That is not your destiny."

I stare up at him through bleary eyes. "What is my destiny?"

"Right now?" Rome kisses my lips. "We don't need to worry about the world or fate or any of it. There is only us. Only this. Everything else can wait. But know this, tré-sur: you are meant for great things."

I can't move under the weight of my grief, so Lucas sets Miracle in the crib and helps me to the bed. "Sleep," Lucas instructs us both, giving Rome his hand and hefting him up. "There are no rabid vampires under this roof. I'm taking Miracle into the living room so the two of you can sleep."

He casts Rome a knowing look that I don't catch the meaning of, but I am too spent to comment on it. "No. Leave Miracle here. I don't want the baby out of my sight."

Lucas is the only one with the gall to stand up to me. He cradles Miracle in his arms. "No dice, Sis. You have to sleep. You're barricading yourself in rooms now. Bedrest means actual rest." Lucas rubs his nose to Miracle's cheek.

"This little bundle of cuteness is going to hang with Uncle Lucas."

Panic rises, but Rome waves Lucas toward the door. "Go on."

"No, wait! Miracle doesn't like to be put down. You can't put them in a crib. And maybe they need to be changed. I can do that."

Lucas shoots me a half-smile. "I see the baby is already calling the shots. Got it. The second Miracle needs you, I'll come in and wake you up. Promise."

I want to protest some more, but I'm not sure I can without revisiting my trip to Crazy Town.

"Go," Rome whispers to Lucas, who obeys before I can say anything more on the subject.

The moment Miracle is out of my sight, I don't know if I have done the right thing. I am exhausted, unable to piece together how wrong this night has gone. My chest begins to jump, my breathing syncopating as my arms stretch toward the doorway.

"Easy," Rome insists. "You look two minutes away from collapse."

After a few stops and starts, my exhaustion takes over and I lie down. The second my head hits the pillow, my body agonizes over how long it took me to get to the mattress.

My hand catches on Rome's when he tugs the comforter up over my form, using only one arm, since his other side is injured. "I haven't even asked you what happened with Fintan." His face is badly bruised, the bridge of his nose puffy and his jaw swollen.

Rome winces but measures his reply. "You got me out. Declan reset anything that was broken. I'm sore, but I will heal just fine. That's what happened."

It's the perfect non-answer because I know he doesn't want to talk about the trauma any more than I am currently capable of hearing it.

Rome kisses my forehead after he slowly takes off his shirt, flinching at the effort even as he kicks his pants to the floor. Then he climbs in and lays by my side in nothing but his underwear. "I'll tell you everything another day. Not now. I just want it to be over. This isn't the life I promised you."

"Rome, I..."

"Sleep," Rome insists. "Sleep. I'll tell you everything another day. Not now. I just want it to be over." He sags against the mattress. "Tell me it's over. Lie to me. I don't care at this point. I just want to sleep."

Though I have precious little solace in me to spare, I flutter my fingers over Rome's chest and give him the only truth I know for certain. "I'm here. I'm right here."

Rome closes his eyes at my promise, then promptly falls asleep.

I watch the man I love for a minute, making sure I can count on the steady rise and fall of his chest before I chase him into dreamland, where surely, they cannot find us.

19

MIRACLE'S MIRACLE

The arguing coming from the living room isn't the best alarm clock, but it wakes me just as effectively.

I have no concept of what day or time it is, only that Rome is in the bed beside me, but Miracle is not.

I am careful with my body this time, taking my steps slow so I can pay respect to the bumpy journey I have endured thus far.

I'm not sure which trauma pains me more right now: the car accident or the childbirth.

The childbirth. Everything hurts, which means I slept long enough to need more medicine to dull the pain.

I don't wake Rome as I study his face in the dark. The puffiness is gone, which I did not expect.

I draw relief from his steady breathing.

He needs more sleep. *Everything will heal*, I remind myself.

I brace myself on the hallway wall as I move slowly to the source of the commotion. My stomach is in agony with every step, along with my pelvis, which feels bruised beyond repair.

I expect the men to be in planning mode when I find them scattered about the living room, but nothing could be further from their minds, it seems.

I gape at the scene unfolding before me. "Nico, what are you doing?"

Lucas is clapping, hooting his approval of Nico, who is walking on his hands across the length of the living room.

At my exclamation, Nico loses his balance and collapses on his head, drawing a bleat of worry from my lips.

"That doesn't count!" Nico protests, untangling his limbs and frowning at me. "She made me lose my step."

"You were just shot in the shoulder like, half a dozen times!" I run my hand through my frazzled hair, wondering just how long I've been out.

Nico pops up and jogs to me, his steps uncharacteristically light for someone who was just captured and tortured yesterday. "Morning, Sis. Want to see how long I can do a handstand?"

My mouth pops open. "Are you insane? You're supposed to be resting your shoulder. You were shot! You were shot loads of times. I know vampires heal fast, but..." My nose scrunches. "How long have I been asleep?"

"Five hours," Orlando replies from his spot on the couch. He's wearing his standard black trousers, but he has foregone his white dress shirt in favor of an undershirt.

Panic slices through me. "Where's my baby?"

Declan points to the bassinet in the corner, luckily far away from where Nico was practicing his acrobatics. "They're sleeping. I would have come and got you if the baby needed you." My brother frowns at me. "Aren't you supposed to be sleeping when the baby sleeps? I thought that's what the book said."

I frown at my brother. "First off, that book was for me to quote to you, not for you to quote to me. Miracle is a preemie! They need to eat every couple hours. I can't be going taking five-hour naps!"

Lucas raises his hands. "You can if I give the baby a bottle midway through your nap. The doctor came by about an hour or so ago. He has no concern about Miracle's lung development, which is good, considering they're still so little."

I harrumph, but apparently the guys covered their bases. "They're really asleep?"

Declan nods. "How are you feeling?"

"Like I've just had a person ripped out of my vagina and then got into a car crash. So, slightly less amazing than usual."

Nico motions to my form. "Well, you look great. I

mean, that hairstyle is all the rage. What do you call that, zombie chic?"

I glower at Nico, who grins at me like the punk he is.

Recognition dawns on Declan. "Ah. You need your pill. Sorry. I didn't want to wake you, but I'm sure the pain probably did."

"You guessed right."

Nico flexes obnoxiously in front of me. "If only it worked on you lowly humans, then you could be doing handstands, too."

I snort at his antics—a levity I wholly did not expect. "I'm not sure that's what the doctor would recommend."

Declan meets me in the kitchen, where we can still see the Nico Show, which apparently is nonstop.

He's got Orlando smiling, so at least there's that.

"What did you give Nico to heal him so quickly, and can I have some?" I joke to my brother.

Maybe I'm joking. Honestly, if Nico can be that energetic and clearly healed in only a handful of hours after such a rigorous session of pure torture, I'm not about to turn something like that down.

Declan shakes his head. "Sleep. Take your pill and then go back to sleep. I'm not sure you want to know all that's gone down in the past few hours."

I quirk my brow at my brother as I take the glass of water and down the pill. "You're only making me want to know more, you realize."

Declan sighs. "I don't know enough about it to make

any hard and fast statements." He motions to Nico, who is trying again to make it from the front door to the far side of the living room by walking on his hands. "All I know is that you are for sure the Last Deadblood, because Miracle's blood did *that* to Nico, who is very much alive."

My eyes widen as my feet move me to the living room, my mouth falling open. Orlando helps me to sit on the couch beside him, not caring that I am in desperate need of a shower and a change of clothes. My big sweetie pie is only snuggly with me, so I never hesitate to cuddle into his side whenever the opportunity arises.

"Watch this," Orlando says, motioning to Nico. "Best entertainment around."

"I didn't know Nico could walk on his hands."

"I'm not sure he could before this whole ordeal. But look at him go."

I watch in awe as Nico walks with purpose on his hands, his legs slightly arced overhead. Most shocking of all is the huge smile spread across his face. I didn't realize he was capable of that kind of joy.

Come to think of it, after all we've been through this week alone, I didn't realize *I also* was capable of joy. Yet here I am, cuddled up to Orlando and giggling at Nico the Clown.

"How did this happen?" I marvel as Nico takes a break halfway to his destination to do a turn in the center of the living room, much to Lucas' amusement.

Orlando kisses my temple, his eyes still on Nico. "The

only variable is that he drank Miracle's blood. They're not the Last Deadblood, Coco. You are." He motions to the bassinet. "I didn't have nearly as much of Miracle's blood as Nico, but I tried a drop to test if that was what healed him so fast, and it did the same to me."

I gape at him. "It did not. If it did, then why aren't you out there with him, walking across the living room on your hands?"

Orlando snorts at the notion, his smile still in place. "Because I'm not a showoff."

"Let me see. I don't believe you. I saw you were shot. I know how long it takes you to heal from a bullet wound. No way are you well enough for what Nico is doing."

Orlando shrugs and rolls up the hem of his pant leg, displaying his calf muscle for me so I can examine the area where I know he was shot.

My fingers flutter over his leg, perplexed and leaning toward awe. "It's not possible."

"Yet because I drank a drop of Miracle's blood, it is. Miracle isn't the Last Deadblood." His arm falls around me as I cuddle into his side. "Miracle is the First Lifeblood." He motions around the room. "We came up with that name this morning. It's really growing on me."

My heart stammers in my chest.

I don't want my baby to have an infamous name, but I guess the First Lifeblood is a far cry better than the Last Deadblood.

20

DECLAN'S HEART

My baby's new moniker rings in my ears, immediately making me want to run for Miracle to make sure they're okay.

"The First Lifeblood." My mouth pulls to the side. "Miracle's blood really did that to Nico?"

Orlando nods, motioning to Nico's acrobatics. "No cure for his bragging, I'm afraid. But physically, he's better than ever. Same as me, and I only had a drop."

I sink into Orlando's side, unsure what to make of any of this. "How about we don't go around drinking infant blood like some sort of sick cult."

Orlando shoots me a dubious look. "You know that's not what it's like. We were testing a theory. I was the control group, since I wasn't taken by the revolutionaries, and I had a fresh wound. I'm telling you, I'm good as new. Declan pulled the bullet out and Miracle's blood did the rest. I have full range of motion, and my body has never felt stronger. Honestly."

His arm around my body is warm and surprisingly inviting, which isn't an adjective I often use to describe someone like Orlando. I understand he is only this way for me, so I take full advantage of the coziness, burrowing my body into his side and making it my haven for as long as safety finds me here.

Orlando seems to understand my need for extra protection, because he pulls me closer, bringing one of my legs to rest atop his thigh. After being in the delivery room with me, my body doesn't have many secrets from him. We were close before that, but now we are positively entangled.

I'm not sure how healthy any of this is. For now, I am relieved not to be snatched at. I tell myself I will examine the health of my relationships later.

For now, I want to be cozy. Judging by the contented rumble of Orlando's chest as my fingernails rake across his stomach, he doesn't mind my close proximity one bit.

Declan grimaces at our closeness after Nico gets almost to his goal and falls on his face. He points between the two of us. "That's weird. You look like Orlando's girlfriend."

"Aw, you love Rome," I comment, still raking my fingers across Orlando's toned stomach.

Declan blanches. "I don't know how you got that out of what I just said."

"You're looking out for him."

Orlando keeps his arm around my shoulders, when usually I would guess a comment like that might give him cause to recoil. "We're mated," Orlando explains. "My body doesn't hold itself back from her. If this is what she needs, I don't hesitate."

I balk, turning my head up at him. "What? Are you serious?"

Orlando chuckles. "Do you think I get all cozy with anyone else? I know this is what you need, so I don't mind it. In fact, it's kind of relaxing."

I frown at his assessment, but I don't have it in me to pull away. "I don't know what to say to that."

"Say it's weird," Declan interjects. "Because it is."

I shoot my brother an eye roll because apparently, I am twelve years old. "Look, I don't care. Just be glad I'm getting all cuddly with Orlando and Rome, and not attaching myself to your boyfriend."

Lucas snickers, rocking my baby's cradle gently. He turns the cradle, making sure I can see my Miracle without having to crane my neck.

This is how recovery is supposed to be, if it can't be in a hospital. I have entertainment in the form of an acrobat, apparently, a friend to snuggle, family to look after my baby so I can rest, and pain that is ebbing, now that the medicine has had a handful of minutes to make its way into my system.

I don't care if our situation is weird. Frankly, this is the most normal thing I've done in a long time.

When Declan and Lucas go back to cheering Nico on when the goofball starts his journey all over again from the front door, Orlando's chin lowers. "Is this normal?"

I shrug, unwilling to examine it all. "You're the vampire. You tell me."

"It feels right, but I am also aware that I am cuddled up to my cousin's wife." A worried look crosses his face. "It's weird, isn't it."

"I don't care," I sigh, my gaze on Miracle, who occasionally opens their eyes to stare at Lucas. "We'll talk to Rome when he wakes. No one's coming for us, right? We can breathe?"

Orlando's arm tightens around me, the fingers on his other hand twining with mine to rest atop my knee. "For now, all is quiet. We wasted most everyone who came to the trade. The only one who got away was Fintan. He'll show his head soon enough. But I got in a shot to his leg, so we've got some time."

I can picture Fintan limping, mostly because I shot him twice not too long ago, back when I was freshly betrayed because I'd thought he was my big brother who cared about me.

Well, I'm not sure I ever thought that. But I certainly didn't realize the depths of all we were dealing with.

I'm sure Fintan has other people in his hovel of horrors. I'm sure someone is in his circle, pulling the bullet from his leg and stitching him up while he formulates a new plan of attack, this time with far fewer teammates.

Fintan sprained his wrist once in high school. I remember him being all frustrated with his limited mobility. He had to rely on Declan and me to help him with his homework. I was quite young at the time, so my help wasn't all that helpful when he would tell me to write something down for him. He whined a lot that month, so much that all these years later, I still remember it.

I can picture him in his navy sweatpants and undershirt, sitting on the couch and sulking while I tried to make the handwriting of my seven-year-old self more pristine so his teacher could read it.

He doesn't have Declan or me to fetch him iced tea or cut his food for him. He doesn't have us to fill in the gaps where his abilities fall short.

He doesn't have a family anymore.

Fintan is completely vulnerable.

Orlando presses the back of my hand to his lips, bringing my attention to the present while Nico walks on his hands across the living room once again. "You look serious. What's going on in your mind?"

I press my lips together in hopes that my cold nature stays trapped inside. But upon my next breath, my jaw tightens. "It's not good enough."

"What? You need something stronger for the pain?"

I cuddle closer, loving the feel of my weight leaned up against Orlando's firm body. "I don't want to sit around anymore and wait for my brother to come after me. Now isn't the time to relax; it's time to strike."

Declan turns his head from the merriment in the center of the living room to stare at me, a quizzical expression tightening his features. "Are we truly the types to go after someone when they're wounded? And not just someone, our own brother?"

"It's either Fintan or Miracle and me. I choose Fintan to take his share of the bullets this time. If we could all survive this, I would say let's walk away and call it a day, but Fintan won't stop, Declan."

"He's got no one," Declan counters. "Orlando shot his accomplices."

"The ones we know about, sure, but there will always be more bigots to throw their hats into the ring on his side. I'm not about to wait around, biting my nails like a damsel in distress, hoping Fintan doesn't find us."

Declan crosses his arms over his chest. "What do you suggest, then?"

I shrug, thinking the decision should be obvious. "Isn't it clear? We need to go out there now and hunt him down. He's vulnerable, Declan. We take him out today so we can sleep in peace."

I can tell Orlando is thinking through my suggestion, which honestly, is really more of a command if I'm being truthful with myself.

Declan is not pleased, his frown fixed firmly in my

direction. "You realize you sound exactly like Fintan, right? Revenge first, sanity never."

I keep my face composed. "I gave up on sanity a long time ago. In all fairness, Declan, you're not the one being hunted."

Declan's brows push together, clearly affronted. "No. My best friend is. I have just as much skin in the game. I want to find Fintan just as much as you do. But I want to bring him to justice. I want him to go to jail so the world can see that vampires have full access to the legal system, and that it will protect them."

My mouth twists as if his words taste sour. "What? But you know that's not how it is."

Declan shrugs. "Why can't it be how it is? This is the perfect time to trust the system. They already locked Fintan up once. He's only free because he escaped. I want people to see that the law will hold people to account for targeting vampires. That is the stronger message than snuffing out the revolutionaries ourselves."

Nico speaks up from where he brought his legs back onto the carpet. He shakes out his arms, his thick black hair sticking up from his acrobatics. "Yeah, but Fintan is after the Last Deadblood *and* the First Lifeblood. He won't be tried for his crimes against vampires. He's a human going after another human, which the justice system has no issue addressing. It's not the statement you're thinking it will be, Declan."

My brother harrumphs. "But a crime against the Last

Deadblood is a crime against the vampires. It's the same thing."

Nico snorts. "It's nothing like the same thing. Though, it's sweetly innocent that you think that. If Fintan went on a tear and murdered five vampires with regular bullets by putting one through our hearts, he wouldn't be held to the same account as he would if those bullets were soaked in Colette's blood. Humans care about their own, and they like to think it's a privilege when their actions look like they care about us." Nico inclines his head to Declan. "But I like the way you think. If more people did, then this world would be a better place."

Lucas keeps his mouth shut, but I can tell he has opinions on the subject.

"Lucas?" I ask him from across the living room. "What do you think?"

Lucas is a good boyfriend, unwilling to go against Declan in front of others, thereby leaving him flapping in the wind with his lone opinion.

Instead of answering me straight, he picks up the newly awakened Miracle and cuddles them to his cheek, a soft smile curving his thick lips. "I think we all did a great job of protecting Miracle. In their first two days of life, they've survived a gunfight and their uncle's abduction. They've been separated from their mother. They've been without me for one whole day," he coos as he brushes his nose across Miracle's. "I wonder what day three will hold, if Fintan gets a say in it."

It's not opposing Declan, but rather spelling the worries out plainly so Declan can see the urgency of what we are dealing with.

I chew on my lower lip, purposefully keeping my butt glued to the couch so Miracle can enjoy their moment with Uncle Lucas before I swoop in like an overzealous mama bird. "I think it would be good if Fintan paid for his crimes. I'm not against turning him in once we find him. What I'm against is waiting around here like chumps for Fintan to come and find us."

Declan rolls his shoulders back. "I can understand that. Can we try to capture him and turn him in?" Declan leans his back against the wall, his head banging to the surface in a self-flagellating rhythm. I can tell he's in a bad place in his mind. "I'm sorry to everyone who wants and deserves a bloody revenge. Fintan is my brother. I know I shouldn't think about that, but he is." Declan closes his eyes, and I can see the pain on his face. "I can't get behind a plan to murder one of my few family members I have left. It's... I can't."

As much as I don't want to be able to understand where Declan is coming from, I won't argue with his heart. His is the only heart that has survived out of all of us. I won't rob him of the vital organ on which we all rely.

Declan's bleeding heart reminds me that I should pay attention to mine, lest it shrivel up and go silent. What's the point in surviving if I have forfeited the best parts of myself?

I can tell by Nico's curled upper lip and Orlando's stiffness that neither of them like this idea.

I take a chance and join my brother out on the ledge where he has chosen to make his stand. "I love you, Declan. I understand."

"I don't," Nico interjects. "Fintan is the reason all of this is happening. He's the one giving bigots a plan to attack us. He kidnapped your sister, Declan! I thought the two of you were close."

Declan bangs the back of his head against the wall over and over again. "We are! It's not that I agree with Fintan or think he shouldn't pay. It's that I want him to pay the right way. Killing my brother doesn't undo what happened to my sister. My conscience doesn't work like that."

Nico snorts his disapproval. "Well, lucky for the world, mine does. I'm all for hunting down the bad apple on your family tree. A single bullet, and this is all behind us."

Lucas' mouth pulls to the side. "That's a little naïve, don't you think? Fintan is one of many who feel that way about vampires. Declan is right; let the world see that the justice system is there for a reason."

Nico shakes his head, still on his knees on the floor. "The justice system had their chance when we caught Fintan the first time and turned him in. The cops turned him loose. They lost him on purpose. Coco was chased out of her hospital bed the day she gave birth because the justice system failed us."

Rome's voice wafts through the living room, spackling

in the cracked parts of my heart with a smooth control that never seems to desert him. "When you stepped out of line, the family decided how to deal with you, Nico. This is for Coletta and Declan to decide. It's their brother, so we will respect their rule."

And just like that, Declan and I have a decision to make.

21

MY FAMILY

I straighten at the validation from Rome that the decision of whether to kill Fintan or capture him and turn him in is the way to go. "Thank you, Rome. You're right. It's our brother, our decision." But I am not capable of making it. Declan is the only person whose heart still beats without foul agenda. "Declan?"

Declan presses his lips together while he thinks things through.

Rome brings himself to sit on my other side, not caring at all that I am wrapped around his cousin. Rome hems me in on my other side, kissing the back of my shoulder so I am wholly cocooned by the Valentino men I adore.

My breathing evens where I didn't realize it was in need of softening. My whole being seems to sigh with relief, having them both as near as possible.

How I need exactly this.

Rome kisses the back of my shoulder again, infusing my body with more tranquility. His fingers trill up and down my arm.

Declan points to the three of us. "For the record, that is distracting and completely weird."

Rome chuckles. "I can't bring myself to care. If my little cannoli has the best man in the world looking after her so it's not all on me? That's a gift I'm not going to turn down simply because it looks strange upon first glance." He brushes his nose across the back of my shoulder. "Did you get your medicine? How's your pain?"

"I did, thanks. It's not as bad as it was when I first woke up."

Rome's hair is sticking up in the back and he has bags under his eyes, but he looks far more healed than he should after being abducted and tortured. I can't even see the puffiness on his jaw, and the bruising from his broken nose is actually gone.

I know vampires heal faster than humans, but I didn't expect...

I gasp at him. "You drank Miracle's blood, too!"

Rome smiles at me, bashful and brazen all at once. I don't know how he does that. "I sure did. If there is anything to get me back on my feet so I can keep the two of you safe, I'm not about to turn it away. I didn't hurt our baby, tré-sur. Honest. Orlando pricked their arm and took a drop of the blood, and I fed off that."

My mouth firms. "Our baby is not a tool or a weapon. Miracle is a baby."

Rome is unruffled by my indignation, his fingertips still moving up and down my arm. "I'll pretend to be sorry, if you need."

I scoff at his churlish offering. "Pass." Insecurity washes over my features. "You're really okay?"

"Better than okay. Tired, sure, but I think that's standard for being a new parent, and also standard for abductions and torture and the like. Apparently, Miracle's blood can't cure sleepiness. But the other stuff is good as new."

"What other stuff?" I ask, my voice meek with worry over what happened to the man I love when he was taken so cruelly from my side.

"They tied me up and beat me. Broke my nose. Broke my jaw. I'm not sure if they broke my leg, but it wasn't working properly. Now it's good as new. Declan reset it and Miracle's blood did the deep cleaning, I guess."

My bleat of agony is swallowed when his lips touch on mine just for a moment.

"Thanks to our baby, I'm good as new. Well, and thanks to Declan resetting my bones to give me a head start on healing properly. Now I can do all sorts of fancy things, like kiss you."

Rome's mouth moves against mine with slightly more pressure to his firm, full lips, but we don't draw out the affection, since we have an audience.

"I don't know what to say to that," I admit. I examine his face for marks, but none are there.

He brushes his fingers over my hip. "Say you're grateful I'm whole and well."

"I am grateful for that."

"Me, too. Miracle made sure that I could take care of you both, is all. Healed all three of us so we can defend the house when Fintan comes back around."

Orlando settles more comfortably into the couch. "Actually, Coco had a better idea. She wants us to go after Fintan now, since he's wounded and hasn't had much time to rally more supporters."

I nod. "I don't want to be afraid he'll come for us. Best take our advantage and hunt him down now." I look to Declan for permission, because Rome made it clear it's up to the two of us how this is handled.

"Non-lethal force," Declan decides. "I'm all about going out and finding Fintan now, but I don't want to be part of anything that murders my brother." He glances around the living room. "If it's any consolation, I would make the same decision about any of you, since you're my family, too."

Yep, that's the heart we all need to go on. No matter how the world has tried to silence or stamp it out, Declan's love has survived, so I make it my business not to shove it in a closet to make room for my wrath.

I nod at my brother. "I can agree to that."

I can feel Orlando deflating, now that sudden death

has been ruled out. "Oh, fine. Rome is right. Fintan is your brother, so we'll fall in line with what you two want. Where do we start, though? I didn't think to keep any of them alive so we could interrogate them. I was just trying to get us all out."

Lucas keeps Miracle where I can see them both, which gives my anxiety the space to see my baby but not have to hover the second we are awake.

Lucas stands near Declan, where the two distract themselves cooing at Miracle.

The pair of them couldn't look more adorable if they tried. I love the look of my brother in love, even when the visual is marred by the grim nature of this current topic.

"Any of Fintan's properties would be a good place to start," Nico suggests, still on his knees. "His restaurant, the loan building, his house."

I nod as I mull over Nico's suggestion. "He doesn't have all that many. That will be a quick check."

Orlando takes out his phone after Declan texts him the addresses of the three properties in Fintan's name. I love watching the plan come together. I love that our families are working on something in perfect synchronicity. It makes me sad that we missed out on all those years in between childhood and now, where we could have been making some real changes in the world if we had only remembered how well we do when we work together.

In a matter of minutes, jobs are divvied up and teams

are assembled, filled in with plenty of the Valentino's loyal men who want nothing more than to see Fintan pay for his crimes against their kind.

When Orlando stands and slides his dress shirt back on, he fixes Nico with an authoritative stare. "You'll stay here and guard the house."

Nico's face pulls. "What? Of course not. Orlando, you need me out there. There are three properties and three of us. I'll lead one of the teams. That's basic logic."

Orlando turns to Rome, who nods, kissing my shoulder before he stands. "We both know you're not going to comply with the Kennedys' wishes. You're going to blow Fintan's head off instead of bringing him in, which isn't the job."

When Nico opens his mouth to protest, Orlando grips his shoulder, giving him a stern look. "I want you to stay with Colette and the baby. I want you to watch the house and stay here. Make sure Fintan doesn't come for them."

Nico scoffs. "Fintan was shot in the leg. He's not going anywhere. He would be suicidal to come here, looking for Coco in the West End."

Rome runs his hand over his face. "Never put anything past a crazy man." He fixes Nico with a serious expression. "I'm trusting you with my wife and my child. It's the most important job there is. Are you up for it?"

Though I can tell Nico still wants to argue, his chest puffs. "I'm up for it. Of course, Rome."

Lucas hands my baby to me, gently lowering the

precious bundle into my arms on the couch. "That's my cue. I need to go to work, kids. Don't commit too many crimes while I'm out." Lucas kisses my forehead. "Proud of you, Mama. That's one perfect baby you've got there." Then Lucas kisses Miracle's cheek. "Don't go missing your favorite uncle too badly, baby bunny. I'll be back this evening."

My heart melts at the cuteness. After Declan and Lucas leave for their day jobs, the Valentino men slide on their shoes and load their many weapons.

I nurse my baby as the guys get ready to leave. To my credit, I don't argue once that I should be going with them.

Rome seems to be thinking the same thing, because when he is on his way out the door, he pauses to kiss me goodbye. "I'm proud of you for staying here. I know it goes against what you want. I know you'd rather be in the thick of it."

I shrug as I move Miracle to my shoulder to burp them. "I'm not all that ready for a high-speed chase. I'm going to give this whole 'being a mom' thing a try."

Rome kisses my cheek and then kisses his baby's cheek next. "Might as well. How hard could it be?"

We share a chuckle at his joke. It's a casual goodbye, like I'm sending him off to work for the day while I stay home with the baby. I don't like to think about what they are going out to do. Bringing Fintan to the police is a gamble, for sure. He already escaped from them once. I am not naïve enough to believe that the last bad apple has been found and discarded. Still, Declan is right; we have to try and trust the system. Fintan will be made an example of, which is the precedent the world needs to see.

"I'll be right here, needlepointing or something really calm. You won't even recognize me."

Rome snorts. "Please let me find exactly that when I get back." He kisses my lips once more. "I'll be back sooner than you can miss me."

"I'll hold you to that."

Rome exits into the garage, leaving Orlando to smooch my lips, which is apparently what we do now. I love the closeness, the affection that is only mine. "Stay safe," I tell him.

Orlando doesn't pander to my nerves. He nods to Nico, handing over the baton of guarding the house, as if it's some rite of passage. I mean, no way is this place on Fintan's radar. He's been shot. The mansion locks down like a fort. Fintan doesn't have much of his backup left, if any, because Orlando shot them all.

And I shot Lampert in the head. I grimace as the visual slaps me in the face. I'm guessing I'll be dealing with that one for many years to come.

But not today. Today I get to be with my baby and have a quiet day at home. With Miracle in my arms, there is nowhere else I would rather be.

Rome will end this, and we will all sleep peacefully.

Or Fintan will escape and gain new followers, meaning he will never stop coming for me.

I take a deep breath and smile at Miracle, rubbing their cheek with the tip of my nose. "You're safe," I promise while Nico moves around the house, checking the locks. "Mommy and Daddy and Uncle Orlando will make sure of it."

ONE FINAL GAME

It's good to know that the years haven't changed Nico and me all that much. He is still terrible at checkers, and I am still a bratty winner.

Nico harrumphs at the board after I jump his last checker. He frowns at me while I wiggle my arms because that is the extent of the obnoxious dancing I can do at the moment.

"You cheated," Nico grouses. "I don't know how, but you cheated. Enjoy your cheating win, cheater."

I keep my hands moving, making up my own insufferable rhythm. "Actually, it's called being better than you. But I don't expect you understand that concept, since I'm better than you, and you stink at checkers."

Nico crosses his arms, grumping like a child.

Of course, I am gloating like a child, so we are evenly matched.

I gather up the checkers and reset the board, turning my head to the bassinet to make sure Miracle is still okay and doesn't need me for anything.

"Is it wrong that I want to hold Miracle? It would wake them up if I did. Still, I miss my baby."

Nico's eyes widen with exasperation. "My gosh, it took forever to get Miracle to stop screaming. You touch that kid, it's your funeral."

I gnaw on my lower lip, trying to be strong. "I want to count the fingers and toes again."

"Ten of each," Nico deadpans.

"It's not fair. You put Miracle down for a nap while I was in the shower. I didn't even get to say goodnight."

"If you wake that baby, I'm going to duct tape you to a chair while I rock them back to sleep." Nico leans back, relaxing into the couch in the massive Valentino living room.

Though, as I live here now, too, I suppose this is my living room, as well.

So weird. I'm still not used to it.

I set the board on the floor and cuddle under the blanket on the other end of the couch. I am grateful for the cozy ambiance and how normal things appear in this moment. We've fought so hard to get here.

"You hungry?" Nico asks me. "I was going to heat something up."

"I could eat."

Nico moves to the kitchen. He is rummaging through

the fridge when I hear the click of the front door. Since the alarm didn't go off, I assume it's Rome or Orlando, come home with their team after a successful manhunt.

But when my head turns, terror trills along my spine.

I mouth my brother's name as his gaze locks in on mine. *"Fintan."*

My gun. My gun is in my purse, which is near the foyer, several feet away. To get to my gun, I will need to move closer to Fintan, which is a bad idea.

My baby. Miracle is obviously in the crib in plain view of my brother. As if on cue, they start to fuss, no doubt sensing my skyrocketing unease.

Terror smites my courage. I am not indestructible. I have a baby I need to take care of. I cannot allow myself to be taken yet again.

Fintan's eyes fall on me, his nostrils flaring. His gun draws up at his side, aimed slightly away from me in warning. He is pale and looks gaunt with lack of care for the injuries he sustained from Orlando. "You're coming with me. Let's get this over with."

Nico doesn't seem to realize there is a person in the house who shouldn't be here, because he starts whistling while he fishes through the refrigerator, just out of sight from the intruder.

I twist the locket around my neck. The heart shape looks sweet enough, but when I twist the two halves of the heart, an emergency pulse goes from my necklace to Rome's, letting him know I am in danger. I don't know how far away he is, but that small motion assures me that help is on the way.

But none of that will matter if Fintan fires his weapon.

Nico's whistling in the kitchen brings to Fintan's attention the fact that I am not here alone. If my brother wants to get at me, Nico will need to be dealt with.

My brother's eyes are wild with purpose, his voice quiet. "You grab the baby and come with me, or I will kill him in front of you."

Fintan's plan is to sneak me and my baby out, which he has to know is not going to happen on my watch.

My voice hits a volume that makes even me wince. "Help! Fintan's in the house!"

Nico drops a bowl of something on the floor of the kitchen and sprints toward me, unsure where the danger is. He draws his weapon, but Fintan is faster.

The bullet sings out through the home, filling the atmosphere with violence I wish I could escape.

I dart to my purse as fast as my bruised body is able while Nico hits the ground.

Nico will be fine, I remind myself. Fintan is out of my blood, so the bullets will only serve to slow Nico down.

I wanted to honor Declan's request to keep Fintan alive and let the system do what it was designed to, but it is clear there isn't going to be an opportunity for me to get the backup I would need in order to get myself out of this alive.

"Hands up, Colette!" Fintan shouts as he limps further into the living room, his gun aimed at me.

I am not about to be taken from my baby, nor am I about to stand still with my hands raised, allowing Fintan to call the shots. I take a chance with my life as I thrust my hand into my purse, my fingers closing around the handle of my gun.

I don't expect my big brother to fire his weapon at me. Maybe I should have, but the fact that I am more valuable alive than dead gave me a false cockiness that I can run in front of a man with a gun and avoid any consequence.

My shoulder explodes with pain so acute; I can't even hear myself scream. I lose my grip on my gun and fall to my knees, holding my wound while I try to reason with a pain that is too great to comprehend.

I hold onto consciousness as best I can, knowing I may not have much left in me that can save my baby or myself.

23

FINTAN'S GUNFIRE

Fintan limps toward me, his expression stern.

"I didn't want to do that. You shouldn't have made me fire on you. At no point do I want this to get bloody for you. I only want to sell your blood. I promised my buyer I could deliver. Don't make this difficult, Colette."

My shoulder is bleeding freely in the foyer while I slump next to the front door, my purse in my lap.

Nico gasps on the carpet, clutching his chest while his body quakes.

I have to pick up my gun, which is still in my purse. I have to put an end to this once and for all.

When Fintan's eyes fall on the crib with my crying baby inside, his shoulders roll back with confidence. "Perfect. If it's a girl, she's about to get a new father. I won't need you anymore. Let the rest of the world fight over your blood. If I have the Last Deadblood, I can raise her as mine and sell her blood as often as I need."

Hot rage is the only thing more intense than the agony of my gunshot wound. My blood heats to a degree that tells me I can lift a truck if that's what it takes to keep Miracle from Fintan's greedy clutches.

"Stay away from my baby," I growl.

Fintan gambles with his life and crosses the living room to pat me atop my head. "Stay here." Then he snickers at what I'm sure he thinks is a funny joke. I'm not exactly fit to go anywhere, bleeding all over the place like this.

He stalks toward the crib, increasing my determination to protect my baby with every step Fintan takes.

I bite down on my lower lip to keep the bleat of pain quiet as I dip my hand into my purse once more. I cannot let Fintan get to my baby.

I can't aim as well as I would like. My arm is shaking as I raise the gun. I hope my shot is far enough away from the crib to give me a wide margin of error that doesn't turn deadly to my baby.

I am sweating. My eyes are lidded from blood loss and pain. My grip is feeble, but that doesn't stop me from taking aim and squeezing the trigger.

I hate this choice even as I make it. I hate that after all I have overcome, this is how my family will end.

The bullet zips through the air, sinking into the back of my brother's shoulder. The force knocks Fintan forward.

I've given my brother a gunshot wound to match the one he gave me.

Fair is fair.

Miracle is shrieking now, the little cries calling for me because there is a scary noise accompanied by a scary man.

Steal me from my family, that's one crime; but steal my baby from me?

I'm not sure there are bullets enough for that.

I cannot bring myself to feel relief at the sight of Fintan's form writhing on the floor beside the crib.

"Never again," I vow as I cock my gun once more. "You will never come for me or my baby ever again."

Fintan gasps a foot away from Nico's body, which has gone limp, no doubt from the pain of being shot. Fintan manages to get to his knees, turning toward me with his gun trembling in his useable hand. "If not me, it will be someone else coming for you." Fintan sucks in a breath through gritted teeth while crimson spills down his arm and puddles on the carpet. "I never meant to hurt you."

Whether my brother meant to hurt me or not isn't a point I am willing to debate. The fact of the matter is I am very much hurt, saved only by Declan, my doctors, and the kindness of the vampire mating bond.

Declan would want me to wait for backup. He would want me to call the police so Fintan can rot in jail, where he belongs. Declan has faith that Fintan can be reformed, and the world can learn from his life lesson.

I do not have the same faith.

The promise that we all made Declan threatens to drown in my apathy, but for the innocence Declan possesses that I desperately need. He believes in justice—in crime and punishment.

I'm not sure what I believe in anymore, so I decide to lower my weapon and bet on Declan, who has never let me down.

I fish in my purse for my phone, calling the emergency hotline to tell them I have found the fugitive whom they have done a half-ass job of searching for. I tell them to send an ambulance without telling them it's for Nico. They won't send one if they know it's a vampire bleeding out on the floor, but Nico has passed out, so he needs medical attention quickly.

I keep my eyes on Fintan, who now has tears streaming down his cheeks. He doesn't look agonized by the pain, but more like the pain has finally brought about a raw honesty in his soul that aims itself in my direction. "I'm sorry," he whispers. "I wasn't there when they beat you over the head. I would never let anyone do that to you!"

"Not because you love me," I remind him, "but because if I'm dead, there goes your meal ticket."

Fintan looks lost, the bags under his eyes nearly purple against the pale nature of his complexion. "Think what you want. If there had been any other way, I would have tried it."

I don't have any more tears. Not for this. Not for him.

My lower lip quivers with rage while my baby screams in the background. "Tell yourself whatever you need. I stopped listening a long time ago." I keep my gun trained on him, though my good arm is exhausted and starting to quake. I need my mates' blood. My health is starting to fade as more blood leaks out of my shoulder.

Fintan's upper lip curls while he holds his wounded arm. "Do it. Pull the trigger. I'm not going to go to jail. I won't do it."

I balk at him. "You want me to kill you?"

"Please, Coco. I owe a lot of people a lot of money. I'm as good as dead when they take me in." He winces through the pain. "It's getting harder and harder to grab you. No one wants to mess with the vampires up close. They won't go through Rome or Orlando to get at you. I'm the only one who can get them what they need, and I failed! They won't let me walk away from this, Coco. I already spent the money. Please!"

The room begins to tilt. "You just got eleven million dollars from me!"

"I have more debts than that. Please, Coco. Pull the trigger." Fintan looks forlorn in his agony, pitiable if I had enough scraps of my heart to put them back together and muster proper emotion.

I lower my gun, knowing Declan is right. Fintan needs to pay for his crimes. His accomplices need to see what happens if I am snatched at, and that it's not worth the risk of doing hard time.

"Screw you," I hiss. "You'll go to jail, and that's that."

Fintan lowers his chin, shaking his head. He motions to Nico, who is still passed out on the floor. "I thought he was Rome. I had one bullet left I was saving for the man who..." He studies the weapon at his side. "I don't suppose it matters anymore."

I don't put together Fintan's words, which make little sense to me. Why break into a guarded home with only one bullet in your gun? That's poor planning.

Not that I'm complaining.

But there wasn't only one bullet in the gun. Fintan shot Nico, but he also shot me.

Fintan presses his lips together, his chest jumping unevenly as determination crosses his face. "Tell Declan I'm sorry."

I cry out when Fintan raises his gun once more. My reflexes are slow and weighted by my blood loss and shock.

I expect the ringing of a bullet to be the last sound I ever hear when Fintan pulls back the safety on his gun. Only this time, he holds the barrel to his temple.

A scream the likes of which I didn't realize I was capable erupts out of me when Fintan's grand finale blasts through the Valentino mansion, ending Fintan Kennedy's life once and for all.

24

ROME'S BROTHER

I am frozen in place, terrified of what I just witnessed. I should have blinked. I should have turned away. As long as I live, I will never be able to scrub the image of Fintan shooting himself in the temple.

My baby is screaming. There's a tremulous quality to the sound, bringing me out of my shock only marginally. My maternal instinct kicks in, forcing me to make my way to the crib on my knees.

I get halfway there and realize I can't make it. I know I am moments away from passing out if I am not careful. I stop by Nico's side, searching his body for signs of where he was hit.

The bullet went into his side, but not near enough his heart to be fatal to him, thank goodness.

"Nico, it's over." I slap his cheek lightly in an attempt to bring him back to the present as much as I am able.

When he doesn't stir, I peel up the hem of his ruined shirt, wondering if the bullet is near enough to the surface for me to just pluck it out. My hand is clumsy and slick with sweat. I wipe any traces of my lethal blood off my good hand, though it's the other arm that is drenched in crimson. I don't want to cause Nico pain, but I figure fishing out the bullet while he's passed out might be the kindest way to do such a thing.

I need to get this bullet out of my own shoulder, but I am hanging on by a thread as it is.

I can't believe Nico is not even stirring. Miracle's cries are making me extra erratic, especially when Fintan's body is lying mere feet away from where I sit.

It feels like an eternity that I dig around in Nico's side, tearing the hole wider than it was.

Still, Nico doesn't wake.

My shoulder feels like it is on fire, coaxing me to lose my hold on sanity, which is feeble at best. I cry out through gritted teeth, though I know I am only scaring Miracle more.

My movements still as I take in the unmoving status of Nico's ribcage. I remove my hand from his side and press two bloodied fingers to his pulse, trying to find some sign that things haven't gone horribly south.

Fintan's words before he took matters into his own hands come back to haunt me. *"I thought he was Rome. I had one bullet left I was saving for the man who..."*

Yet Fintan had at least two more bullets in his gun after he shot Nico.

Terror races through me afresh when the cruel nature of this dark reality shakes me to my core.

Fintan had one bullet for Rome.

Reality slams into my chest so much that it knocks me back.

Fintan had one bullet coated in my blood. He was saving it for Rome, but Nico took the final blow instead.

"No! No, Nico! Wake up! Nico!" I lean over with a scream of agony and perform mouth to mouth, pumping my good hand to his sternum while I blow air into his motionless mouth.

My baby howls for me. My brother's body continues to bleed onto the carpet. My own blood loss causes my vision to blur.

None of that matters right now. Nico can't die. Not after all we've been through. The road to get here was bumpy and filled with regrets. This was supposed to be our chance to start fresh, to be a family.

Time has no meaning anymore as I pump air into Nico's mouth to no avail. "I'll let you win at checkers!" I promise him, fighting with my breath as it grows shallow. I give him another puff as I press on his chest with my paltry strength. "I'll give you the last cannoli in the fridge! Please, Nino-bear! Please!"

When the front door bursts open and Rome races in with Orlando on his heels and a slew of vampires loyal to the Valentino family, I know my attempts have done nothing to resurrect my Nino-bear.

I don't stop my pathetic attempt at CPR until Rome pulls me off his brother.

"Don't look!" I shout. "Don't look. Go, Rome! You don't want to see this."

When Rome takes in the span of Nico's unmoving body, a gasp that breaks my heart rips through the air.

"No! Nico, no!" Rome drops to his knees just as I did, pumping his hands to Nico's chest just as futilely as my attempts. His face is determined, his eyes rounded with a craze that he will undo this permanent loss by sheer force of will.

When Orlando rounds the couch to take in the scope of the damage, his hand goes over his mouth.

My grief is one thing, but I cannot stomach Rome's trauma. Not if there is a way to save him from it, even slightly. "Orlando, get Rome out of here!"

Orlando is frozen where he stands, in complete and total shock at the carnage that accumulated while he was away. "How did... What did..."

"Fintan shot Nico with the last bullet he had that was coated in my blood. Fintan thought he was shooting Rome! Then when he knew I was going to send him to jail, Fintan put a bullet in his own brain."

Miracle screams at the recap. As much as it pains me to hear my baby cry like that, my saving grace is that the baby is safe and didn't see any of the disaster from inside their bassinet.

My baby didn't watch their uncles die.

Orlando stands in the center of the living room, unable to bring himself to get Rome out of here so he doesn't have to see the sight of his brother, dead on the living room floor.

"Nico!" Rome shouts, all reason leaving him just as it did me.

It's not until the front door opens and Declan's form fills the doorway that reason comes back to me in fragmented bits. "Coco? What happened? Rome called us to come home. You're bleeding!"

My lower lip quivers. Fintan's upper half is splayed on the ground, but from where Declan stands, I don't think he can see more than Fintan's legs. "Declan, if you love me at all, you will turn around and wait outside."

Declan's mouth sours. "What? I'm not leaving when you're bleeding."

"An ambulance is on its way. I can wait. Out. Now."

Declan shakes his head. "What happened?"

"Declan, go!" I shout, then gasp at the pain my outburst caused me.

Orlando comes to life. He spins around and shoves Declan out the door, locking him out so Declan doesn't have to see the graphic sight of Fintan's body in such disrepair.

Declan won't see Fintan dead. He can keep what is left

of his dreams, and hopefully they won't mutate into nightmares. Declan's heart has to survive. His is the only one worth saving at this point.

An ambulance is on the way for me. I knew this fact, but saying it aloud to Declan makes it true.

The relief is more than my body can withstand.

When a sigh escapes me, my vision blurs and then goes dark without negotiation, no matter how hard I try to stay conscious.

The last thing I know is Rome's agony as he pumps without stopping atop his dead brother's chest.

It doesn't matter that Rome has survived; part of me knows we will never recover from this.

25

RESTING AND HEALING

The hospital is quiet, I'm guessing largely due to the fact that the entire wing has been cleared out to take care of us.

My shoulder is done for, at least for the time being. Apparently, all you have to have is a gunshot wound, and if you're the Last Deadblood, you get a whole team of doctors and the best care in the world.

If you're a vampire, however, you get nothing.

When I first came to and realized Orlando had sustained an injury while he was out that he'd had to stitch up himself, I started tearing out the stitches on my shoulder until they tended to his injury with the same care I received.

That hadn't gone over particularly well, but it was effective.

My baby finally gets their fair time in the hospital,

being fawned over by the nurses who do all they can to make sure we get the care we need. They make a show of using proper pronouns, which I appreciate.

Orlando sits in the rocking chair by the window. "You feeling okay? Want to rip out any more stitches?"

I cast him half a tired smile. "I'm good. Don't say I don't know how to throw a tantrum."

The hospital is quiet, but not creepily so. We have new guards sent by the governor, along with flowers and a promise that she is working to make the world safer for vampires. Though I know we might never be completely safe so long as there is ignorant hate out there, today there is no sense of impending doom.

That's a first for me.

Orlando checks his phone before his gaze returns to the crib by my bedside. "Lucas says that Declan is eating now. Just crackers, but it's something."

I nod. "That's good. It's been two days since it all blew up. He needed to get something in him. Tell Lucas he's wonderful for taking Declan away from it all while the press does their thing."

"I'm sure I used those exact words."

Life is so much different when I have the correct amount of medicine in me. I can move without immediate pain, which is no small triumph.

Best of all, Miracle is resting. My baby doesn't have to think about the fact that their Uncle Fintan and Uncle

Nico are dead, nor that the world is still trying to figure out language for the new addition to our family.

It's no matter. The world will make room for us because I will make it so.

Orlando points to my face. "You've got that stubborn look about you that's going to cost me another bullet hole, isn't it."

I settle into my pillow. "Just hoping that was our last gunfight ever. Any word from Rome?"

Orlando's gaze shifts away from me. "I told you I would let you know if I had any news about him. Nothing yet. I've got people with him."

My worry spills out of me before I can hold back the tidal wave. "He's never needed time alone unless he's checked out. He just went through a trauma."

Orlando nods. "You both did. We all did. No one won this thing."

I breeze past his assessment that I should be included in the level of grieving that he and Rome are in. Mine is nothing compared to theirs. In fact, mine is nothing at all.

I know that should be a red flag that slows me down, but I can't think of that right now. I'm just glad to be safe.

I fidget with my blanket. "I hate that Rome is burying Nico alone. I should be there."

Orlando shakes his head. "No. You should be right here. Exactly here. In that bed. Rome knows what he needs. He's a big boy, Coco."

"No, he's a lost boy. He just lost Nico because of who I am. He shouldn't be alone. We shouldn't be apart."

Orlando tilts his head to the side. "You're really thinking you should be anywhere but here?"

I chew on my lower lip. "Rome just lost his brother. I should be there for him. Wherever he is, that's where I want to be."

Orlando runs his hand across his scruffy chin. "You just lost your brother, too. I think we all need a breather."

I settle into my pillow. "Oh, fine. You realize this is messed up, right?"

Orlando shrugs as his phone rings. "What else is new?"

He answers the call, cuts his eyes my way and then stands, taking the call in the hallway.

Nothing ominous about that.

Miracle starts fussing the moment Orlando moves out of the room. I make to lift my baby from the crib, but that is something I need help to do, given I have one functioning arm.

Stupid Fintan.

That is how I have decided to deal with my grief. I will dismiss it as if it is a gnat that buzzed out of turn. I will grieve for Fintan when I finish being angry at his choices that led him to his demise.

I'm not sure that day will come, but if it does, I will be sad then.

I wish I could have been with Rome when he buried Nico, but that was something he wanted to do only with

Orlando. The three of them have spent their lives fighting hard to redeem the people of the West End.

And Nico did not live to see us cross the finish line, which always seems to be moved just out of reach.

When Orlando returns a handful of minutes later, I don't even address the large box in his hands. My bleat of distress is aimed at the crib by my bedside, because my baby needs me, but I cannot get them in my arms.

Orlando sets the box down in a rush, compensating for what my soul craves. He lifts Miracle from their crib and hands them to me, helping me get situated using my one functional arm. He moves a pillow under my elbow, so I have some support. "Is that better?"

I exhale a hefty portion of my anxiety. "Much. Thank you."

"You can call the nurse, you know."

I nod but don't consider that an option. "I know, but I don't want to risk it. I have a short list of people I trust near my baby."

Orlando studies my face as I try to situate my gown so I can feed Miracle. "I guess it's going to take a long time before we can tempt fate with luxuries like trust."

Maybe we're coming out of this jaded, but we survived. Even if I have to forfeit the better parts of myself in the exchange, it is worth it because I have a true Miracle in my arms. "I'm okay with the wait."

Orlando steps back and taps his finger to the box he brought in. "From Ming Lu. The governor is coming by as soon as the doctor clears you for visitors, and she's bringing reporters. Ming Lu thought this would photograph better than a hospital gown."

I don't even have to look inside the box to know she is right. "What does the governor want?"

Orlando shrugs. "A photo op with the baby? No idea. You know more about politics than I ever care to."

I motion to his pocket, where I know he has stashed his phone. "What's going on with Rome? You looked worried."

Orlando's mask of indifference is not quick enough to conceal the concern plaguing his eyes. "Oh, nothing. Just my cousin being his charming self. When he gets here, act... I mean, maybe you won't be as horrified as I was when he told me. Whatever you do, remember that we're all a little fragile right now. We're not making our best decisions."

My optimism plummets, immediately going to worst-case scenario.

"He's injured," I guess. "Who hurt him?"

Orlando shakes his head. "No one would dare mess with us now. He's physically fine."

My next guess comes out hollow. "He's gone. He decided this was too much work, so he split." I try to compose my face. "It's fine. I'll figure it out."

Orlando swears. "It's nothing like that, Coco. Man, you've got a bleak outlook. He's come up with an idea, and I don't like it. That's all."

"Is it dangerous?"

Orlando resumes his spot in his rocking chair by the window. "The opposite of dangerous, actually. He met with the governor this morning. He's already making plans to..." Orlando stops himself short and shakes his head. "I don't want to get into it."

I glower at Orlando. "You're killing me with this cryptic talk, you realize. Just tell me already."

Orlando mimes zipping his lips. Then he throws the invisible key into the air and shoots it with his imaginary gun.

Only my big sweetie pie can make a childlike gesture grotesque.

When I am ready to stand and Miracle is safe in Orlando's arms, I call the nurse to help me in the shower. My pride has severely diminished, now that I can barely do anything on my own.

The shower is slow, but we manage.

After I emerge, I stare in the mirror of the steamed bathroom, looking and feeling a little more myself. The bruising from the car crash has gone, but the stiffness lingers. My shoulder will need weeks before I can even remove the sling, I am told. The main thing that is slowing me down was the lack of aftercare when I gave birth. But luckily, I am in a safe place now, where I can take my time healing in the company of a medical team who can compensate for my many shortcomings.

The nurse helps me with the gown that Ming Lu sent over.

I was expecting something maternal, perhaps a pink dress with white polka dots.

Ming Lu does not believe in holding back. She is ever dressing me to be a beacon of hope. Even though the governor will be visiting me in the hospital, I am certain the backdrop of medical accoutrement will be all but forgotten when this dress is in the scene.

The pure white dress goes down to my knees, flowing around my waist with plenty of space for my post-birth body. The thing is lined in gold around the outer edges, making me look like a warrior victor of the past. The cleavage dip is incredibly low cut, and laces with gold ribbon, so I can nurse without tugging too badly at my gown. The shoulders are tied with that same gilded ribbon, so the doctor can tend to my shoulder without me having to disrobe.

The material is soft yet thick enough that I feel confident having my picture taken without the world seeing every nuance of my body that is, quite frankly, none of their business.

The whole ordeal of showering and getting dressed takes me an hour. When I emerge, I am greeted with the surprise of Rachel and Victor, grinning at me with silent cheers, because Miracle is asleep in Orlando's arms.

Orlando catches my eyes that tear up at the sight of these amazing stylists. They took a chance on Mayfield and placed their bets on my vision of a better future. "I figured you couldn't do your own hair the way you would want it, what with your shoulder busted up."

The three of us hug because we have not seen each other in far too long. For all the politicians who claimed they wanted to make a change for the marginalized people of the world, it was my small team of stylists who truly shook this city and showed them how to be brave.

"Fourteen businesses," Rachel tells me. "Fourteen businesses in Midtown now have signs that read *'Humans and Vampires Welcome'.*" Her grin is made of pure sunshine and hope. "It's working! The world is changing, Colette."

Optimism rises in my chest. This was my goal so long ago when I moved back to Mayfield. This was what I wanted.

Now that it is happening, I almost cannot believe it. The gift is too grand to comprehend. "It's really happening?"

Rachel nods and then opens her travel bag. "It is. But all of that talk is for another day. Right now, it's you time."

Amid my gushing of gratitude, I am sat down in a chair while Victor and Rachel get to work on a pretty bleak "before" model that needs some severe work to truly shine.

By the time the governor arrives with a cavalcade of reporters and security, my hair has been trimmed and styled to perfection. Victor didn't hold back any of his skills accomplishing the complicated top knot that has curls and twists tucked against the sides of my head.

Rachel did a facial, then tended to my makeup and

nails, all the while promising me that the salon is thriving, and I don't need to worry about a single thing.

"I hired our first vampire stylist," she tells me, filling my heart near to bursting.

That was the goal, and she did it without me having to push the whole thing uphill by myself.

I am not alone in my quest to bring peace to Mayfield. Perhaps I have never been alone; I just needed to see the proof for myself.

I adore Rachel and Victor. Their care is civilizing. I have felt much like a rabid woman, trying to hold onto a semblance of sanity, lest it leave me forever. Self-care is a buzz word that is often dismissed as a luxury and not a necessity, but after all I have been through, I can confidently declare that I very much needed one whole hour of goodness aimed directly at me.

When Rachel and Victor leave, Orlando sets the baby in the crib so he can help me into the bed. After all the drama and trauma, I am not about to leave this hospital bed until the doctor kicks me out.

The world can deal with itself for a while. I have done enough.

26

ROME'S PLAN AND PROMISE

When the governor is announced an hour into my afternoon nap, Orlando sits me up, warning me not to take the baby out of the crib. "If you wake that baby, I will take all the pins out of your hair."

I harrumph at him, but heed the logic of not waking a sleeping baby.

Of course, that is a moot point when eight people swarm into my room, taking pictures and spouting out questions at whatever volume they feel like.

It is a testament to Orlando's control that he does not draw his weapon when the baby cries. Instead he scolds them all and shoves them out of the hospital room, leaving only the governor and her assistant, Lacey.

Their congratulations are far more respectful of the fact that there is a baby in the room.

Orlando holds Miracle while I carefully explain the sex of the baby to the governor.

To her credit, she asks only clarifying questions and promises to educate herself so she doesn't have to burden me with queries she could find the answers to on her own.

I am calm until the door opens once more, revealing the one face I have been longing to see. "Rome!"

The visage of the man I love has been marked with bruises or exhaustion for much of the recent times I have seen him. Today, he has showered and shaved. His dress shirt isn't wrinkled, though that isn't the thing that shocks me.

"You're wearing a blue shirt!" I exclaim like an accusation. "I've never seen you wear a color before. It makes your eyes shine." I marvel at the sight of him. "My gosh, you're beautiful."

Rome smirks at me, knowing exactly how dapper he looks. "Thought I would dress up to see my family." He shakes the governor's hand and nods to Lacey. From the way they greet each other, I get the feeling they have conversed recently.

The governor stands back while Rome kisses my forehead. "Should you go first, or should I?" she asks him.

I glance between the two, unsure what is going on. I look to Orlando for answers, but he turns his chin so as not to give anything away.

"Okay, people. What gives? What did I miss?" Panic rises up in me. "Is Declan okay? Is it Lucas? Who's hurt?"

Rome sits on the side of my bed and sandwiches my hand between his. "Everyone is doing well. One day, good news won't look like bad news to us."

I tilt my head at him. "You have good news? I haven't seen you in days."

Rome kisses the back of my hand in apology. "I was taking care of a few things, but I'm here now."

"What kinds of things?"

Rome glances at the governor. "I think that means I'm going first."

The governor smiles at the two of us and steps back, as if she is making herself invisible so Rome and I can have a private moment.

Rome seems to be at peace. I never thought I would see that look on his face without it being snatched away, but there it is. "I buried Nico," he starts. "Orlando and I gave him the respect he deserves. He was cremated and his ashes sprinkled in our backyard, so he is never far from home."

My heart aches for the sad end to a long journey. "I would have held your hand through that. I'm so sorry, Rome."

Rome shakes his head. "I'm glad I had some time to think." He presses his lips together as if searching for the right words to come to him. "I don't want my whole life to live and die in Mayfield. I don't think I can take it another minute. We've done all we can here. It's time to let others take up the cause and run with it. Change can't always come from us. It has to be widespread, otherwise we are fighting a losing battle." He brings my knuckles to his lips again, this time speaking so I can feel his words touch my skin. "I want to move out of Mayfield with you two. I don't want our baby to think this is the best humanity can do. I want them to have a bigger view of the world. I want their dreams to be grander than ours."

Pressure builds behind my eyes. "You want to leave Mayfield?"

Rome nods. "Not an hour or two away. I want to move a whole continent away. I want a fresh start. I want hope."

A tear trails down my cheek. Though I know my goal was to stay in Mayfield to be a conduit for change, with the revolutionaries broken up and several businesses in Midtown catering to humans and vampires now, perhaps it is time to pass the baton.

I squeeze his hand. "I would go anywhere with you. I don't care where. Somewhere that Miracle can have friends and play without fear of being snatched at." I lower my chin. "But you know you can't travel to a different continent. The world hasn't changed so much that they are going to let a vampire get on an airplane and move out of Mayfield for good."

The governor steps toward us, keeping her voice low. "That's where I come in. Your boyfriend and I have been talking about the future, and I decided to bring a few of my friends in on the conversation." A smile of one delivering important news comes over her as she slides her hands over her navy suit. "The Prime Minister of Lonmure has sent you a formal offer to be the delegate in his country to speak on behalf of vampire rights and human re-education on compassion."

Rome finishes her grand announcement. "The thing is, he knew you wouldn't accept if it would mean leaving your baby and me behind."

The governor inhales, rolling her shoulders back. "Effective next week, the ban on vampires flying overseas will be lifted. The ban on vampires owning property outside of Mayfield will be lifted. If you accept this position, you will need to live in Lonmure so you can advocate for a system that can better serve the needs of the vampires who might now be able to travel there."

My mouth hangs open in shock as the perfect puzzle pieces line up to create a vision of the future I never could have imagined. "What did… How did… You did all this in a few days?"

The governor nods while Lacey grins at her side, shoving a clipboard in my face. "This is the formal offer. Lonmure is ready to lead the way to change, and the governor is prepared to follow."

I take the clipboard and read over the job offer in silence, acutely aware that four people are watching me.

"This was my mother's job," I whisper. "She did it here, but it's the same job, even if it's overseas."

Rome's hand rests on my knee. "I am ready to leave

Mayfield, tré-sur. I am ready to be the first vampire in Lonmure."

I close my eyes as the life laid out before me swirls in my mind's eye.

I can see it all, perfectly posed and ready for the taking.

The revolutionaries will lose steam because they would have to fly across the ocean to get at me.

Mayfield is beginning to see the consequences that come from segregation, and it seems they are ready to start the baby steps forward to construct a brighter future. Governor Mason can watch over the city to keep them on track.

There is no more halluci-blend plaguing the West End. The vampires have a chance to heal, now that they are not being sabotaged.

The police force has largely been let go and replaced with sympathizers to the cause.

Not everything is fixed, but we have a chance.

I can see my Miracle laughing and playing as they grow into the force of nature all the people in my family line came to be.

I can see it all.

When I open my mouth, the wrong thing comes out. They want an answer, not an obvious observation. "You're wearing a blue shirt," I announce to Rome.

Rome glances down at himself. "You're focused on that after all we just told you?"

I shake my head. "You really are ready to leave

Mayfield behind." I set down the clipboard and reach out to hold his hand. "Yes. Let's do it. I accept. I want you to be the first vampire in Lonmure. I want to follow in my mother's footsteps." I smile as I turn my head to my big sweetie pie. "I want to dress Orlando in all sorts of colors, too."

Rome lowers his chin while Orlando's expression firms. "Orlando is going to stay in Mayfield, little cannoli. We can't leave the West End to the mercy of Mayfield. One of us has to say behind and keep an eye on things. I spoke with Orlando about it earlier today, and he accepted. He said if I agree to go, he will stay and run things in Mayfield. He will be the head of the Valentino family so I can leave town and, well, have a family."

Horror slashes my features. "What? No! No, we have to stay together. That's not going to work."

Orlando's voice is rough with emotion he won't display in view of the governor and her assistant. "I'll send you with more than enough of my blood to sustain you. And I will fly out once a month on the jet the Prime Minister will send for me."

My mouth drops open. "The what? I didn't see anything in there about a jet."

Orlando keeps his eyes on Miracle. "Transportation is included. That's the military jet. Rome made sure that was in your offer, so your health doesn't suffer."

I gape at the verbiage. "Are you serious? You can really live away from me for a whole month? Not to announce my codependency too loudly, but I can't go a month without being near you, Orlando! You're my mate! You're my..."

Orlando dons a brave expression. I know he is just as torn up about this as I am, but he is being an adult about it.

That makes one of us.

"It'll be hard, but you have Rome, who is also your mate. I'll come to you once a month for the first year until I find someone I trust enough to hand over the West End to. After that, who knows? You might just find yourself with a permanent third wheel in Lonmure."

Just knowing that his plan isn't to leave us forever separated eases a portion of my angst. "Your goal is to come to Lonmure and live with us?"

Orlando nods. "It'll be a rough year, being apart, but if the Valentinos are going to leave Mayfield, we have to do it right. One hard year, and then you'll never be rid of me."

Rome holds my hand. "And we'll have to fly back to Mayfield all the time, too. You're a delegate, which means you have a foot in both countries. We'll see Orlando far more than once a month."

Another tear slides down the apple of my cheek. "Do you promise?"

Rome holds my hand to his face. "I promise you now that you will live a long, happy life. And we will make sure that our people are granted the same thing we finally have. I promise there is hope we can rest on that will not be taken away."

I lean my forehead to his, knowing that if Rome Valentino gives his word, he will make good on his promise.

Mayfield will have its guardian angel, and I will do all I can to pave the way so possibility is a promise we can rest our heads upon.

"Then take me there, Rome. Take me to that future you swear exists."

Rome smiles as he kisses my lips.

In that small exchange I can feel the world changing, opening up in new ways to make room for all the good that has yet to unfold.

EPILOGUE

$\mathcal{I}$ gape at the picture Orlando shows me on his phone. "That is inappropriate. No, Orlando. Just no."

My big sweetie pie frowns at the picture. "It's a perfectly fine tree house, Coco. I built it myself. It'll withstand even a tornado."

I refocus on the mirror and secure the final curl in my sophisticated updo. "I'm sure it will, but Miracle can barely walk more than a few steps at a time. They are years away from being old enough to climb up in a tree house."

Orlando shoves his phone in his pocket. "Well, when they are old enough, it'll be ready for them. They still like red balloons, right? Because I don't want to go through the pony debacle all over again."

"Yes, Miracle is enamored of red balloons."

"Good. I filled their bedroom with fifty."

I gape at him as I straighten my corsage. "You filled their bedroom at the Valentino mansion with fifty red balloons."

Orlando grimaces. "Anything less than fifty felt cheap. And I put them in the playroom, not their bedroom."

I shake my head. "I can tell you're still competing for favorite uncle."

"Lucas keeps trying to edge me out. Did you see that he got Miracle a sandbox? I mean, a sandbox. Come on."

"The monster," I joke. My nerves are a little on edge, but thanks to my regular dose of medicine from my mates, my hands have never been steadier. I lean up and kiss Orlando's cheek. "Miracle loves you, and so do I. Rome, however, might have a conniption when he sees the tree-house. Fair warning."

Orlando grumbles under his breath.

I stand, straightening my fitted tuxedo. Ming Lu is up for any challenge. I didn't realize a tuxedo could be sexy and form-fitting on a woman, but this getup is hitting me in all the right places. "Am I showing?" I do my best to suck in my stomach, but I know that's a losing battle.

Orlando's palm migrates to my midsection at mention of baby number two. "You look perfect. No one will know until you're ready to tell them."

In the year since Rome and I left Mayfield for my new job as a delegate to Lonmure, a lot has changed, and yet by the same token, much is the same.

Mayfield has its share of discrimination that it needs to

repent of, but there is now a blanket policy that no businesses are allowed to exclude vampires any longer.

The streets are safer, thanks to the eradication of halluci-blend.

All medical personnel are now trained in vampire healing as part of their education, though admittedly, that flaw in our history still has a ways to go before I will call it true progress.

But the reason I am in Mayfield for the second time this month is because today is a day that I have been waiting for oh so impatiently.

When the door to the dressing room opens, I smile at my brother.

Declan was less himself after we buried Fintan beside our father and mother, but Lucas made it his mission to see my brother smile again.

The proposal half a year ago really tipped it.

"You ready, groom-to-be?" I ask him, marveling at how dashing my brother looks in a tuxedo.

Declan's hair has been trimmed, and Victor gave him and all the wedding party a shave this morning. After waiting for this day for this long, I have spared no extravagance.

Today is my brother's wedding, and everything will go off without a hitch, so help me.

Declan smiles at me, slightly winded. "Ready as I'll ever be. Your boyfriend gave me this." He holds up his right hand, his eyes wide. "I don't know what to do with the Valentino family ring! Does this make me all bossy and scary?"

I snort at the thought. "You know, when I think of you, those are the two adjectives that come to mind."

Declan mimes a laugh as he looks down at the ring. "It was Nico's."

My heart clinches in my chest at the heirloom that twines our two families together that much more. "You alright?" I ask him.

Declan clears his throat, then takes a deep breath. "It's you we should be worried about. You sure you can walk me down the aisle in those heels? I'm afraid you'll break your ankle."

I swat at him. "Don't jinx me!"

Declan snickers. "You're nearly as tall as I am with those things on."

"That's the goal. I'm giving you away. I need to appear authoritative."

The harp music wafts through the open door, reminding us that banter should be saved for the reception, when we don't have people waiting for us.

Lucas' father is giving him away, and Declan asked me to do the same for him. We are walking in on either side of the rows of seats, where the grooms will meet in the middle to exchange their vows.

We practiced this three times last night. If anyone forgets their cue, I will throw a fit. This is my brother's special day.

It will be perfect.

Orlando leads the way to the back of the chapel, acting as the usher. He kisses my cheek and slaps Declan's palm three times before he goes out and walks slowly down the aisle in his tuxedo.

My big sweetie pie isn't one for festivities and formalities, but for Declan, it seems we are all willing to bend a bit.

Declan's smile survived. At the end of the day, that is the thing that has given us all hope.

So Orlando dressed himself up in a tuxedo for Declan. He parades down the aisle without a fuss because Declan his just as much Orlando's brother as he is mine.

Rome holds Miracle, who scatters flower petals from their basket where the rings have been tied. I don't harbor the same panic I used to whenever Miracle is more than two feet away from me. That took a lot of therapy and a whole year of no one snatching at either one of us, but finally we got there.

Miracle won't have an overprotective, crazed mother.

That's the hope, anyway.

The few people we have kept close are in attendance, making the affair elegant and intimate.

The chapel is decked out in about a thousand lilies because Lucas said once that he liked that flower. There are white satin draperies to give the guests the impression that nothing sordid has ever befallen our family.

I have never been one to settle, and I plan on passing

that high standard on to my brother, starting with the most beautiful wedding he could ever have hoped for.

I nearly choked him when he uttered the word "courthouse."

No. This is cause to celebrate. We are getting another Kennedy. We are adding a wonderful person to our family, ensuring the future will be far brighter than our gruesome past.

"I'm nervous," Declan admits. "And I look weird in a tux. How is it Rome looks like he was born to wear one, and Lucas looks like a million bucks, but I look ridiculous?"

"You look like a spy who doesn't take crap from nobody. You wear that ring and that tux well, Mister Kennedy. Perfectly handsome." I blink up at him, my arm through his while we wait for Miracle and Rome to reach the front of the chapel. "You're getting married, Declan."

Declan's eyes widen as if this is just now dawning on him. "Oh my gosh. I'm getting married. It's really happening."

Our wonder turns to joy as we break from our formal demeanor so we can hug through the happiness that comes when the world has space for you.

"I never thought this day would come."

I close my eyes as I rest my cheek on his shoulder. "I did. Some days, it was the only thing that kept me going. Knowing you could have all this—a wonderful future with a man who deserves someone as amazing as you? I needed this dream to come true."

Declan's eyes glisten as he pulls out of the hug when the music shifts, sending us our cue. He grimaces at my lapel. "I messed up Mom and Dad. They're crooked now."

My corsage has two white ribbons on either side of the lilies on my lapel. On the ends of each one is a small portrait of my mother and my father.

Together, we will walk Declan down the aisle. Declan will have the brightest of futures; we have made certain of it.

When the doors open and the guests all stand, my brother and I take our first step forward to usher in the beauty of a new era.

For after all we have sacrificed, two things are certain: love is love, and peace is possible.

Love the book?
Leave a review!

Enjoy a Free Preview of *Sins of the Father*, book one in the Sinfully Sacrificed trilogy

27

SINS OF THE FATHER

Sweating

*D*on't let them see you sweat.

It was good advice from Daddy when I was off to my first big modeling job, but I'm not sure I can help the trail of moisture creeping down my spine.

"Arlanna Scarlett Valentine, I'm Officer McGregor," booms the voice at the front of the classroom.

Well, I was told it was a classroom, but I highly doubt we'll be studying classic literature in here. Given the sewing machines bolted into each desk, I'm guessing we'll be learning one thing only: manual labor.

It's all I can do not to wince at the sound of my full name. I'll bet everyone else in here only had their first and last name announced on their first day at Prigham's Penitentiary, but thanks to my family's sordid reputation, I get the middle name treatment.

The no-nonsense, yet not overly aggressive guard, points to an empty desk in the very front of the room.

Super. Everyone's going to be able to stare at me while I fumble through this. I've never used a sewing machine in my life.

Head held high, I remind myself. It's one of Sloan's credos that's always served me well. I miss my bodyguard more than anything or anyone else. He would know what to do in this situation, with too many eyes studying my every move as I walk to my new desk.

The concrete mocks me from all sides. I'm used to lush carpet and drapery of the highest quality. The floor here and four massive walls are all unpainted grey. A chill radiates from them as if they're trying to send a warning that no warmth can survive inside of Prigham's Penitentiary.

Going from Sloan being never more than three feet from me at all times to suddenly being miles and miles away is enough of a shock to my system. Standing in front of everyone, looking every bit the prisoner I've now been sentenced as, adds a whole other level of impossibilities. And the worst part is that I'll be facing this alone.

How I wish I could duck away from the hundred or so gaping stares that find me in the too-bright classroom.

Not a class.

Workroom.

I stayed away from new people throughout most of my life. It was too difficult to maintain real friends in a life where private tutors kept me indoors and gossip columnists waited outside our gates, rabid for a picture or a morsel of something they could spin for their readers. I'm not often around so many people my age. Looking around, just about everyone here is in their twenties or thirties, and I'm smack in the middle at twenty-eight.

Of course, from the acclimation class I had to complete after I was sentenced, I knew as much. We're all children of criminals. Our parents have paid a sum to the government to have their sentences passed to us—their offspring—instead of doing the time themselves. That window only happens if the child is in their twenties or thirties. After that, they can't pass their crimes off onto us. We're in our peak physical ability right now, so we'll be put to work.

Starting with sewing, apparently.

I never dreamed Daddy would do this to me. The Sins of the Father bill was only for people who hated their children and led despicable lives. Daddy loved me.

I feel so stupid for believing that.

Whispers splinter out like rippling waves around the room. Though they're all doing their best to gossip behind cupped hands, their choice words lap at my resolve.

Mafia princess.

Conan Valentine's daughter.

Four-Thousand-dollar stilettos.

Criminal.

Had it coming.

I roll my shoulders back, refusing to cower. It didn't faze me when the judge hurled many of those same words my way; it's not about to make me trip over myself now, even if I've had to trade my famous stilettos for steel-toed black work boots.

I can feel at least ten sets of daggers staring my way now. They stick out because everyone else is more curious than spiteful. The ten glare at me as if it's *my* fault their parents ran with the inventor of the criminal element— a.k.a. dear old dad.

They've been waiting for me to get sentenced. I can see it in their conspiratorial glances.

Head held high. Head held high.

I'm wearing the same utilitarian, shapeless orange jumpsuit they all were issued, but the stigma of my family's name infuses a shudder in many. I've long since learned to live with the mix of respect and disgrace that people associate with being a Valentine. It earned me the shallowest of friends out in the real world, and in here, it's going to earn me enemies at every turn. I can already spot a few of them now, and I haven't uttered a word.

That's the power of the Valentine name.

Head held high.

I make my way to the desk I'm assigned, and Officer McGregor follows me. His blue pants and matching uniform shirt demanding respect, even if he drags his heels while he walks.

Neither of us are counting on someone sticking their boot out and tripping me. My knee hits the ground, but it's when my chin bashes on the edge of a desk on my way down that my eyes begin to water.

Well, it sure didn't take long for things to escalate from glares to physical contact.

Tears bloom from the smarting pain, but I refuse to let them touch my cheeks.

I turn to glare at Officer McGregor, who was a foot behind me and didn't reach out to keep me from falling.

Message received: I'm on my own.

"Alright, alright. Keep it together and make the lunch guards deal with your daddy issues. This is work time, Malrick." Officer McGregor makes a show of helping me up, frowning at the offender—a guy maybe my age whom I don't even know. He wears a sneer, not any sort of remorse.

Sounds about right.

Daddy's got a wide reach. There's no telling how many families he's screwed over and gotten their kids sent here.

The officer takes a look at my chin, which I'm pretty sure is bleeding. I know it'll be bruised. "Jeez. Not a great first day you're having, eh?"

As if it's my fault some idiot tripped me.

He grimaces at the damage done to my face. "You need to go to the infirmary?"

I touch my chin. It's only a few drops; nothing too horrible. If I'm not supposed to let them see me sweat, then I'm pretty sure I'm not supposed to freak out over blood, either. "Days spent acclimating or taken off to go to the infirmary don't count toward time served, so no, thanks. I'll work, if it's all the same to you."

Officer McGregor purses his lips, and then nods appreciatively, his short brown hair barely moving. "Fine by me."

"Could I get a napkin or something I can throw away to staunch the blood? Wait, this'll do." I glare at the jerk who tripped me, swipe some blood from my smarting chin and smear it through his blond hair. "Thanks. Malrick, is it?"

I make it a point to let him know I'll remember his name. I was raised right. I know it's important I show the class that my blood will always come back to haunt them.

It's Daddy's way.

Officer McGregor crosses his arms, staring down the two of us as the room goes silent. "Are we going to have a problem here?"

Malrick stands, folding his arms behind his back while he glowers at me. "No, sir."

He's my exact height of five-foot-eleven, but I do what I can to appear taller.

I miss my heels.

My posture suggests I'm a giant to be reckoned with. Status or not. Stilettos or not. Bodyguard or not, I won't be messed with. "So long as Malrick will help staunch any blood so I don't ruin my new uniform, I don't have a problem. That sound fair?"

Officer McGregor lets out a chuckle, but then coughs,

as if he didn't mean to let his amusement be known. "Fair enough, Arlanna Scarlett Valentine." He draws out my whole name, but this time, it feels like respect, instead of infamy-by-proxy. Then he reaches over and rips the orange sleeve off Malrick's forearm, eliciting a groan from him.

Malrick rubs his wrist. The black cuff we all wear in here to mute our magic is something I'm not sure any of us will get used to. "I'm going to get a demerit if the afternoon guards see my uniform damaged like that."

The guard shrugs. "Demerit for a damaged uniform, or I can have you thrown into solitary for fighting again. You're getting off easy."

My eyes narrow at Malrick, letting him know he got away with this once, but I'm no pushover. "What a gentleman," I say airily, dabbing my chin with his orange sleeve.

Officer McGregor's hand on my shoulder is heavy. He turns me from Malrick before more swagger ensues, and directs me to my desk. He presses his thick finger down atop the binder next to the sewing machine. "You'll start every workday by picking up the manual and reading through your instructions. If you have questions, I'm at my desk."

The clear vibe I get from this clean-shaven guy in his late forties is a solid, "Don't have questions."

I can respect that.

Though, truly, I don't have much choice in the matter. Everyone who works at Prigham's Penitentiary that I've met thus far has been no-nonsense types with tasers and batons on their belts. I know better than to cross them.

I should probably be intimidated, but the sight of Officer McGregor's stalwart expression only makes me homesick. I didn't even get to say goodbye to my bodyguard. I wonder if Sloan misses me, or if he's glad to be rid of the shopping malls I dragged him through. If he's been reassigned to someone else, will they even care that Sloan loves strawberry shakes? Most of the guards who work for the family are trained to have no personality, and not ask for a single thing. But Sloan's been by my side since I was born. Will his next charge remember his birthday? Will they even know he prefers strawberry tarts to regular old birthday cake?

If I'm not there, will anyone care to remember his birthday at all?

He'll probably be shuffled through Dad's organization, stuck driving around some self-important lackey who uses Sloan's intimidating presence like social currency. He'll become a prop, not a person.

But he's a person. Most days, Sloan was my *only* person. If there's a word for an uncle who's also your best friend, that's Sloan.

But in a world where parents have the option of paying a sum to the government for their children to do time for their crimes, I have precious little hope of seeing Sloan until I serve my father's sentence.

Five years for getting caught running an illegal gambling ring.

And for being an accessory in the death of a cop.

And being "mysteriously" tied to too many shipments of Luster Oak.

That's not too bad. I'm twenty-eight. I can't imagine I'll miss that much in the real world by the time I turn thirty-three.

At least, that's the lie I tell myself to get me through the day.

I flip open my manual and keep my eyes on the pages, willing the burn of unshed tears to go away.

Sloan will be fine. When I get out, I'll bake him five strawberry tarts to make up for his five crappy birthdays without me, and it'll be like this never happened.

Except it's happening right now. I'm three days in, and it's already felt like a month.

But this is the first day after I've been acclimated and shown around, and I'm expected to start earning my keep.

Thank you, legalized slavery. Sure, I'll sew you whatever I'm supposed to be making.

Except I've never operated a sewing machine in my life.

Page one has a detailed layout of my machine, listing each part and its name, so if something goes wrong, I can more quickly identify the problem area. Everyone else is sewing away, and I'm surprised to find pockets of pleasant conversation splintering out all over the place.

So apparently, we can talk while we work. That's good

to know. Many of them even move their desks closer together and form little circles, their machines humming away while they sew in straight lines.

Officer McGregor's black boots are kicked up on his desk. He's leaning back, leafing through a paperback western, as if he couldn't care less about the noise, so long as we all do our work.

I like that.

Well, I normally would like that, except here, I don't have friends. I'm persona non grata.

I stick my nose in my instructions and do what I can to follow the diagram for threading the ancient gray contraption. It's actually a lot more complicated than the "simple method" the binder brags about.

I mess up the thread six times before a desk slides toward mine. The dark-skinned girl beside me is probably around twenty-six or so. It's hard to tell. Her natural black hair stands out about four inches in spindly, tight curls, showcasing her kind eyes and gentle smile. Her freckled nose scrunches as she makes a face at my machine, as if scolding it for giving me a hard time.

"I'm trying to follow the instructions, but I can't seem to..."

She doesn't say a word in response to my fretting, but gently takes the thread from my fingers and slowly shows me that I've been missing a hook near the top of the machine, which the thread must catch on if it's going to do its thing.

Once the contraption is threaded, she flips a page in my manual, frowning. Then she points to the bottom corner, then to the bottom corner on the next page.

I groan at the small numbers. "A page was torn out? That explains it. Thanks. What's your name?"

She reaches over and fishes a charcoal pencil from her desk, then writes on the edge of my manual.

I squint at the sideways scrawl. "Charlotte? Is something wrong with your voice?"

"Vow of silence," comes an answer from two desks down.

I peer across the way, but the woman with shoulder-length straight black, silky hair doesn't look up from her machine.

I glance over at Charlotte. "You've taken a vow of silence? That's pretty heavy. Any particular reason? Silence until you're free again?"

Charlotte shakes her head and flips the page in my manual, indicating I should ask her if I have any questions about the machine once I get started.

"Silence until she knows how to set us *all* free," the other girl explains, still not looking at me.

I gape at Charlotte, unsure what to do with something so noble and entirely impossible. "You're not speaking until you've got a plan for setting *everyone* here free? How close are you on that?"

Charlotte holds her hand level to the floor and tilts it from side to side.

Her spokesperson answers for her. "Charlotte doesn't believe children should have to pay for the sins of their parents, no matter what the law says. She's been silent for two years, focusing her energy into healing the judicial system."

What the actual...

"Wow. I don't think I've ever heard of anything so bloody impressive. Good luck to you." Then to her friend, I ask, "What's your name?"

"I'm Cassia Chang. You might want to figure out your machine. We've got a quota to meet. Let the new girl be, Charlotte. She can figure out the rest on her own."

The fact that Cassia hasn't once looked at me sinks in my stomach. "Gotcha." She doesn't want to be associated with me, because I'm likely to be targeted until the disruption of my arrival at Prigham's settles. She doesn't want to catch any fallout.

Smart girl.

I dab at my leaking chin with Malrick's sleeve scrap, steeling myself to get through this day without further incident.

But Charlotte doesn't move her desk from its new spot beside me. In fact, she scoots her desk closer, motioning to her machine, so I can follow her silent hands-on tutorial.

Man, I want a friend. Just one person with whom I can share exasperated sighs.

But it's clear Cassia speaks for Charlotte, and she doesn't want the two of them associated with me.

"That's okay. I'll figure it out. You're not exactly going to win any popularity points, sitting this close to me."

Charlotte casts me a wry look, and then crosses her eyes to bring out a smile on my face, giving me the impression that she couldn't care less what anyone thinks of her or her affiliations.

Okay, now I *really* like her.

Charlotte's hands move slowly, giving me time to mirror her actions as she positions the soft pink material. She presses the pretty sides together, and leaves the faded insides facing outward.

When I finally get it right, Charlotte grins in time with Cassia's harrumph. "Oh, fine." Cassia ambles her desk across from ours, connecting her gaze with mine. "But if Charlotte gets backlash from helping you, I'm holding you responsible, Princess."

"You and everyone else," I mutter, training my focus on the work at hand.

I will not feel sorry for myself. I will not wallow. I'll let myself feel it all when I'm out, in five years. Until then, I'm going to make clothes for... I flip a few pages, but don't find the information I'm looking for. "What company are we making these for?"

Cassia stares at me for a few beats, as if waiting for the irony to build. "These pants are Natalia's Secret."

I gape at Cassia, who sits with her knees far apart, like a cowboy. "Are you serious?" My stomach churns.

My contract with the designer brand was ended

prematurely because of my incarceration. I've been the face of Natalia's Secret since I turned nineteen. Their underwear line was designed with me in mind.

And now I'm sewing the clothes I've been modeling.

Bile rises in my throat. "Natalia's Secret slacks cost nine hundred dollars a pair! And they're being made by inmates for eight cents an hour?"

When I learned the hourly wage in acclimation, I'd laughed out loud. Now I want to throw my desk across the room in protest.

Cassia's jaw sets with all the things she probably wishes she could voice, but no one wants to hear. "You say that like slave labor should be frowned upon. Like companies using us to make their products for practically free is wrong. What's so terrible about companies profiting off of people who have no choice but to work for them for barely any pay?"

Immediately, I like Cassia, and forgive any sandpaper that's come about in her personality.

A snicker slips through my lips, and the corner of Cassia's mouth quirks while I engage in her ire-laced banter. "Sounds admirable to me. They don't have to waste their time paying people a fair wage out in the real world who claim they need jobs to feed their families. Less paperwork, not having to deal with unions and whatnot. Smart."

Cassia grins, but doesn't look up at me.

I'll take it.

I feel completely foolish, modeling clothes made by legalized slave labor. I should have researched more, done more digging before signing on with a company who would do something so despicable.

But I can't change that now. "Regret is a useless emotion," Daddy always says.

I wonder if he regrets sending me here.

We work in silence for a few minutes until something dings at my hair, followed by several sniggers. I curl my lip in the offender's direction. "A spit wad, Malrick? Seriously? How old are you? I thought you had to be at least twenty years old to serve time at Prigham's."

"Malrick," Officer McGregor drones, not looking up from his novel.

"Sorry, sir," Malrick replies, sounding nothing even close to apologetic.

I fish the gross, damp bit of rubbish from my long chocolate waves, silently bemoaning the fact that I won't see my hairstylist for five more years. "I sincerely hope this is as close as any woman's come to wearing Malrick's DNA," I mutter to the girls.

Charlotte shoots me a look laced with compassion, and Cassia softens. "Just ignore him, Arlanna. Ignore them all. Everyone here is a different shade of miserable, being stuck how we are. Some of them like to take it out on each other, since we can't punish our parents for sending us here."

"Arly," I correct her. "Arlanna's my name for the papers. The people I like get to call me Arly."

Cassia smirks and then jerks her thumb to her chest. "Cass. Welcome to Prigham's, Arly."

And for the first time in a long time, I finally feel like I found a friend.

Maybe even two.

Read *Sins of the Father* today!

ABOUT THE AUTHOR

USA Today bestselling author Mary E. Twomey lives in Michigan with her three adorable children. She enjoys reading, writing, vegetarian cooking, and telling her children fantastic stories about wombats.

While she loves writing fantasy, dystopian, and paranormal tales for her readers, Mary also writes romance under the name Tuesday Embers, and cozy mysteries under the name Molly Maple.

Visit her online at www.maryetwomey.com, and sign up for her newsletter, so you never miss a new release.

www.ingramcontent.com/pod-product-compliance
Lightning Source LLC
Chambersburg PA
CBHW010319100726

47906CB00006B/1050